GLAMOUR EYES

JESSICA LYNCH

FOREWORD

The **Wanted by the Fae** duet is written as a set of companion books to my **By the Fae** universe, specifically **Touched by the Fae.** When the reader first meets Callie and Ash in the prequel short, *Favor*, they've already been mated a while, plus they've had a child. But as their child—Riley/Zella—went on to deal with the Shadow Prophecy and find love with a Dark Fae of her own, I knew I always wanted to go back and show how these two met—and why a guard in the Fae Queen's Court would choose to give up everything for his human mate.

This is that story (or the first half of it, at least). It's the one that starts it all. The one that brings an arrogant Light Fae male to his knees all because of a pretty girl with a gaze that can look right through him *and* his glamour.

So happy reading, and I hope you enjoy the first part of Callie and Ash's story! The second half will be out in a few months, so while this ends on a cliffhanger with the couple separated, *Glamour Lies* will show their HFN *(Happy For Now)* since *Favor* definitely throws another wrench in their relationship—on the plus side, following the events of **Touched by the Fae** (after the Fae Queen is no longer a threat), Callie and Ash have definitely earned their HEA!

xoxo,
Jessica

"I see dead people."

Callie Brooks wasn't really a fan of horror movies, though she'd sit through them. Suspense flicks, too. She didn't like to be scared and couldn't understand why people put themselves through that *on purpose*. But when Mitch settled on watching last year's biggest hit for movie night a couple of weeks ago, she'd been too tired to argue for her choice. She'd rented *Bring it On* from Blockbuster, so glad to have snagged the last copy, but Mitch came home with *Sixth Sense* and she reluctantly agreed.

After all, she argued for *Coyote Ugly* over his choice of *American Psycho* last time. It was his turn this go-round.

To her surprise, she actually got into it—mainly because she felt for the poor kid. *I see dead people...*

Callie knew exactly what that was like. Change *dead people* to *faerie creatures* and that could be the tagline for her entire life.

Shoot, even the child psychologist part was dead-on. Except, you know, for her doctor not being dead. Dr. Forrest was no Bruce Willis, and while the old dear tried her best to help Callie with her visions, she didn't understand.

No one did.

Which was exactly why, one day, Callie just... stopped. She stopped reacting, she stopped being afraid, and she stopped telling her parents about the *things* she saw. So long as she acted like she couldn't see them, the creatures left her alone. Her parents backed off with the doctor appointments. And Callie could pretend that she was normal.

Pretend, of course, being the key word there.

It seemed to work out so far. Callie was twenty-two now, living in the city, working as a budding photographer. Well, she processed and developed film at Buster's Photo, but her boss—the infamous Buster— let her hang up some of her prints and she even sold a couple. As far as Callie was concerned, it counted.

Hey, she might as well use her sight to her advantage. When she could see things that no one else did, it showed up in her work, making her photographs something unique—and she wasn't just saying that. Even Buster admitted that she had the sight.

Whenever he said that, Callie laughed. Poor guy. He didn't know the half of it.

While her favorite types of shots were candids, unless she got her subjects to sign waivers, she couldn't put them up for sale. That was fine with Callie. She was able to shoot photos just for herself—considering it practice—while using her photographs of scenery to pull in some extra cash.

People in the city really got a kick out of her nature shots. She figured it had something to do with being surrounded by asphalt and skyscrapers and trucks belching black smoke everyday. The lush green of the grass, the vibrant blue sky, the towering trees... her customers loved it, especially when she told them that each picture was actually taken inside of the city.

Not too far from Buster's, and within walking distance of her apartment, there was a park that Callie considered both her haven and her sanctuary. It was a total tourist spot, but she didn't mind. She'd grown up in a happy home with her parents and two older sisters and, now that she was basically on her own, she liked to be a part of the hustle and bustle of the community while still being able to return to the quiet of her apartment after.

While she considered her roommate her closest friend, Mitch was a workaholic. Callie worked full-time hours for Buster, but her hours were early: from six am to one pm, five days a week; she was a morning person, and sometimes even went in an hour earlier with Buster's permission to process her own film off the clock. Mitch, though? He worked more than fifty hours in an office, doing some kind of dot com thing that she didn't understand. Good thing she didn't have to for Mitch to be able to pay his portion of the rent on time.

He kept telling her that he was working toward a promotion. The new job came with a huge pay raise. That, coupled with Callie's occasional sales, could mean they'd be able to get a better apartment as the two of them finally started to make it big in the city. And, sure, Callie knew that Mitch was trying to one-up his older brother—who happened to be married to Callie's sister, Ariadne—but so long as they had a roof over their head, she was content.

Content... that was a good way to describe Callie these days. It had been an adjustment, leaving the suburbs behind for the city, especially since she caught sight of far more *other* beings mingling in the city crowds than she ever did back home. The way she saw it, though, it was just further practice for her to keep on acting as if she *couldn't*.

Most of the time, she pulled it off.

And then there were times like now.

It was a bright summer afternoon, and Callie had already pulled her full shift at Buster's. It was a good one. She had a line on a sale: one of Buster's buddies who seemed drawn to a photo Callie had taken of a particular tree in her preferred park at the beginning of spring. Between the dandelions sprouting in the dew-covered grass, the faint shadow falling behind the tree that highlighted its strange shape, and a robin caught mid-flight, it epitomized the previous season.

He had promised he'd have an answer for her during her next shift, and if he leered a little as he kept her hanging, Callie just managed to hold onto her smile. He wasn't the first customer to flirt with her or imply that he'd throw money at her for one night in her bed. She was a pretty young woman who knew it, and who also made no apologies for it. She drew the line at taking money for something that wasn't for sale —when it came to bed partners, she was choosier than her sex drive probably appreciated—but if he kept her on the hook, it only seemed fair that she could do the same.

Especially when the older gentleman mentioned in a completely *not* off-handed way that he might know someone willing to give a young photographer a shot at her own showing...

And all because he saw something in her spring photo.

Now that it was summer, she thought she might make a series of it. The tree itself was in an unusual spot. Set apart from most of the much taller oaks that bordered the park, this one was half the size, a totally different species that Callie hadn't been able to identify. Maybe because it was blackened and twisted, nature turning it into something other than it was supposed to be.

Kind of like Callie.

There was a bench that was sat catty-cornered from the tree. In the spring and the fall, it was often occupied since there was nothing nearby, and no tree to provide shade. In the winter, the wind blew right through anyone sitting there, while the summer sun left anyone daring enough to take a seat blistering in the heat.

Callie didn't care. She was grateful it was empty when she arrived since that gave her a place to set down her camera bag and set up her supplies. Besides, knowing this was her plan, she covered her fair skin with sunscreen, leaving her long, white-blonde hair to settle over shoulders as she sat down on the edge of the bench before glancing over at the tree. She wanted to make sure that none of the other park goers had laid their blankets beside it, or were sunbathing near it.

A glance, and then a double-take.

The grass was empty. But standing next to the tree, in a bright patch of sun, was the most beautiful man she'd ever seen before in her life.

No, she corrected an instant later. Not a man—a *male*. Because while he appeared human, he most definitely wasn't.

He was *other*.

It was only fitting that he was standing in the sunlight since he seemed to absolutely gleam. With skin the color of rich bronze, he had a tan that must've been ingrained all the way down to his bones. The long, silky-straight tawny hair falling like a sheet down his back made his skin seem even darker. And his eyes...

They were sun-colored too, a striking golden shade that almost flashed as his head cocked in her direction. It was that flash that made her so sure that his unearthly irises would appear so shiny. She'd never spied this male before, but she'd seen a couple of his kind—and she'd never been able to stop her instinctive reaction to get the hell out of there.

Stunning, but dangerous. A perfect predator—

A lump lodged in her throat right as her eyes locked on his.

Uh-oh.

—and she was snared in his trap.

For the first time in years, Callie forgot her number one rule: don't let the faerie folk know that you can see them. She learned long ago that it was easier that way, and it kept her both safe and sane.

Hoping he hadn't noticed the way she stared, she ripped her gaze away from him, unsettled that it took more of her willpower than it should. She moved her camera bag over, fiddling with the zipper, ducking her head while she peeked back at the tree.

Out of the corner of her eye, she watched as the male faded out of sight, leaving behind a vaguely hazy patch that, now that she saw it, she couldn't ignore.

He was standing by the tree, but now he wasn't. From the recognition low in her gut to the gleam of his sun-colored eyes, she knew he'd never even been in the park.

He hadn't even been in her *world*.

Faerie. He was in Faerie, but his gaze had settled on her anyway.

Because of course it did. The one downside to being able to see things that most humans couldn't? That which she saw always seemed to sense in some way that she was different. That she could spot them even while they were trying to hide behind magic and glamour.

Callie swallowed the lump in her throat, the image of that stunning male seared into her mind.

When she was a little girl, she thought of the fantastical creatures—some that looked like people, most that didn't—as strange but ordinary. Then, when it became clear that no one else could see them, she was convinced they were imaginary. After too many years of therapy and even longer where she took it upon herself to make sense of the things she saw,

Callie eventually accepted that they *were* realer than she ever would've imagined.

But they were magic, too.

Compelling.

Otherworldly.

It was the most accurate description, in a way. The creatures that crossed the veil between worlds visited the human world from Faerie, a fantastical realm where unicorns might exist but trolls and dwarves and fairies definitely did.

Even from across the park, she could see the thin haze that separated the two worlds. All of her research books—from Yeats's *Fairy and Folk Tales of the Irish Peasantry* to *Fairies for Dummies* and everything in between that she could get her hands on—made it clear that there were weak points between worlds where the realms were kept separated by a barrier as thin as a veil; hence the name. They were usually found marked by fairy rings or stone circles, some sign that the land had been touched by a faerie creature.

It seemed as if, in this park, the veil was marked by a tree that was nearly split in two, making it look like a fondue fork. The rectangular-shaped patch of hazy space hovered right beside the charred side.

City lore said it had been struck by lightning decades ago, but suddenly Callie wasn't so sure. Whatever happened to it, the sunbeams filtered through its droopy branches, drawing her attention back to the hazy patch.

To the hazy patch, and the gorgeous male who had blinked back into her sight.

He seemed closer, as if he was traveling through the veil, prepared to cross from his world into hers. And maybe if there hadn't been that moment when their eyes locked before, Callie could pretend that he wasn't focusing on her.

In her experience, it was never a good thing to draw the attention of a Faerie dweller. Especially the more humanoid ones. The monsters were absolutely dangerous, but if they even risked crossing over into the modern world with its cars and its computers and its tech, it was a pretty safe bet that all they wanted to do was cause chaos and hunt. The tricksters and domestic fairies were kind of similar. Brownies, redcaps, goblins... so long as you didn't get snared by one of their traps or offend them, you were fine. Nowadays, with the world moving on from the old ways, most of those lesser fairies didn't even bother crossing over since very few still believed in them, let alone respected them.

But the humanoid ones? Callie might be immune to their glamour and their charm courtesy of her "gift", but that didn't mean the faerie wouldn't try to compel her anyway if she caught their attention. From all her research, those types of faeries were stronger, more powerful, and less easy to fool with her pretending.

Worse? She'd seen hundreds of Faerie-touched creatures since she recognized they were *other*. But this guy? She'd never seen anyone quite like him because, God help her, she was drawn to him in a way that had her grabbing her camera bag and, as casually as she could, climbing up from the bench.

If she wanted to head toward him even when she knew she shouldn't, that was a pretty big clue to get out now.

Especially since it appeared he was drawing closer and closer. If her gut was right—and it had never steered her wrong before, even when her mind refused to accept what was directly in front of her—then he was coming for her.

No, thanks.

She slung her camera bag over her head, letting it settle against her chest. Struggling to control her suddenly frantic breathing, she busied herself with searching in her purse for a few seconds before swallowing again and casting her gaze over the park.

Like before, she forced herself to sweep right past him, as if she couldn't see him at all. Hopefully he thought her earlier surprise was a fluke, that she hadn't met his stare in such a heated way on purpose or at all.

Tossing her long hair over her shoulder, Callie forced herself to stroll away from her bench, heading leisurely toward the sidewalk. She didn't turn around, though she did look behind her. Out of the corner of her eye, she caught a flash of gold that winked on the edge of her vision before vanishing.

It could be a trick, she told herself. She forced herself to keep walking, smiling at some of the regulars on their afternoon walk, even pausing to pet a friendly pup she usually saw playing frisbee with his owner. Only when she was heading out of the park did she dare one last peek over her shoulder.

Callie let out the breath she didn't even know she'd been holding when she saw that both the male and the patch of *other* was gone.

Phew.

2

I t was a punishment.

At least, Melisandre intended it to be a punishment. The Fae Queen, ruler of both the Seelie and Unseelie Courts of Faerie, had recently decided that he was not allowed to serve her as one of the elite guards that lived in her grand palace. He was banished to his rooms at the guards' barracks instead, and given a post out of her sight while she fumed over his perceived insult.

Ash hadn't mean to upset the queen. It was just his bad luck that he was the guard standing to the right of her throne when her glamour slipped; as the queen, her command over her glamour was impeccable, but it tended to waver whenever one of her court had the poor taste to mention Melisandre's missing consort, the former Summer King. For a few moments, her blonde curls darkened to black, her yellow eyes shifting to silver, her tan fading as she turned her pointed stare on the Seelie noble who should've known better than to utter Oberon's name.

Ash had protected his queen. With a soft cough, he snared her attention, gesturing to her suddenly pale skin. He never knew why Melisandre insisted on appearing as a Light Fae when she was a royal from the Winter Court, but she was the Fae Queen and he owed her his loyalty the same way as he served Oberon when he sat on the same throne.

Too bad that his queen turned her ire on Ash as well as Raine. At least only one of them was destined to stand frozen, another statue for her endless summer garden. Raine's wealth and his pedigree couldn't protect him from Melisandre's cruelty down to the way she sentenced him with an innocent smile before she sent Ash from her sight.

At the barracks, Ninetroir pointed out that every member of the guard knew better than to respond whenever Melisandre lost her temper. While her glamour slipping was rare, her quick temper wasn't, and Ash brought this punishment on himself.

He wasn't standing as a statue to amuse the queen, but his new assignment wasn't too far off. For the next decade or so, he was sent to the edge of the realm, guarding a point where the veil between Faerie and the Iron—the human realm—was thin enough to be a concern. It wasn't quite a fairy circle or a pocket of shadows, but there was a risk that fugitive faerie folk might try to escape their fate in Faerie by slipping through the weak point. Worse, a human might cross over on their own without being led by one of his kind.

A human that hadn't been controlled by the touch? They wouldn't last for long in Faerie, and Ash had heard stories about what his fellow fae would do to be the one to take that first touch inside of Faerie without having to brave the Iron. He didn't blame the, since he'd done worse himself in his time.

Though he rarely paid any attention to the mortals on the other side of the veil, he'd touched a fair amount of humans during his three centuries. Between his glamour and his charm, it didn't take much to convince them to give him permission to touch them anywhere he wanted to. And Ash would—he *had*—all for the rush of power that a gifted piece of soul gave him.

It had been decades since he played with a human pet, though. About the same amount of time since Melisandre had last sent him to the edge of the veil.

Nothing much changed, he concluded as he stood at his post. Fashions did, and the amount of iron humming in the air was so strong that he could just about sense it even through the thinning veil. The last time Melisandre grew annoyed at him and sent him to the borders, it had been a different post, but the view was basically the same. The greenery, and the humans milling everywhere, unaware that they had one of the Blessed Ones in their midst.

Though he stayed firmly in Faerie, Ash pulled on a layer of glamour that would keep him hidden in case any of the humans noticed the weak point between worlds. He was the only fae responsible for this post, and he knew better than to question Melisandre when it came to his punishment.

Eventually she would calm down, and she'd fall back into her "benevolent ruler" role, oblivious to the fact that many of her subjects referred to her rule as the Reign of the Damned. Until then, Ash would have to stay out of sight and hope that she was still far more furious with Raine.

He didn't expect much to happen during his guard duty. His previous tour along the borders lasted close to two decades and in all of that time, the only interesting thing happened when a Dark Fae nearly burned to a crisp when he got caught in the Iron during the time of no shadows. Ash had wondered if it was worth rousing himself out of his ennui before crossing over and dragging the lifeless male into Faerie. He saved Ninetroir then, earning a life debt that he carried with him always just in case he ever needed to call it in.

Ash didn't expect to be entertained during this tour, and only hoped that the Fae Queen's grudge didn't last as long. Until then, he would do what she commanded of him. When the alternative was a queen who took her buried aggression out on the statues that lined her garden, a fae who valued his immortal life obeyed his queen.

No matter how intolerable it was to be this close to humans.

Cloaked in his layer of glamour, Ash drummed his fingers against the hilt of his sword while watching the humans through the veil. Sound didn't carry through, but he could see clearly to the other side of his post.

And that's when he noticed that one of the humans was watching him back.

Ash's fingers flexed; instead of tapping the hilt, he had the sudden urge to draw his sword. The weight of her curious stare made him react in a way he didn't expect—or appreciate.

The human female could see him. Despite the veil, despite his glamour, her eyes were locked on him. And, for the first time in a long, long while, Ash found himself attracted to a human.

Her hair was long, as long as his, though it was such a fair color, he would've said it was white. Even from the distance, he could see the tops of her rounded ears poking through the soft-looking strands. Definitely human. Beautiful, too, Ash mused. He didn't normally go for the human look, but maybe she had a touch of faerie blood in her because he'd never seen a mortal with such a lovely face before.

And she could see him. He was almost sure of it. This human could see him.

Did she have the sight?

Only one way to find out.

It was daylight in the Iron. As a Light Fae, Ash could cross over into the human world and suffer no consequences so long as he returned before the sun set and the shadows came.

Deciding this strange human counted as part of his duty to protect this entrance into Faerie, Ash started toward the border.

Even before he passed over, he knew he was too late. With his first step, she rose from the bench she'd been seated on. With his next, she was already gathering her belongings. By the time he pushed through the veil, she was gone.

Ash patted the hilt of his sword in barely stifled frustration before returning to Faerie, the white-haired beauty a mystery, but one he dismissed as soon as she was gone and he was home again.

A human, he scoffed.

He needed to find one of the courtesans and get laid if he thought he was attracted to a human.

WHEN NIGHT FELL in the Iron, Ash left his post.

He headed straight for the barracks where he

had his own space, surprising himself when he joined some of the other soldiers for a meal instead of going to the nearby inn for fairy wine and a willing female. When he first realized where his portal had taken him, he thought about conjuring up another until the pretty human's face flashed in front of him and he chose to head toward the mess hall instead.

Only because he wanted to, of course.

The next sunrise, he returned to his post, knowing that the veil would show him that same patch of nature he'd watched over the day before. While magic was fluid and one spot of Faerie didn't quite coincide with the same spot in the Iron, the weak points were like anchors; they were fixed. Until Melisandre relieved him of his duty, he was destined to stare at the same human park.

Which meant that there was a chance no matter how slim that he might spy the white-haired female who had haunted his dreams.

He hated her for that alone. She was mortal, a nothing to someone like Ash, and it was almost an insult that she had transfixed him with only the quickest glimpse. He wanted to believe it was only the way she locked eyes with him, almost as if she could *see* him. That her quick escape, like she was trying to run away from him, made her more than just another mortal.

At least, he told himself that as he waited to see if she would return.

She didn't. Not that day, or the next. Hours blurred together, as they often did when he was on a pointless assignment, and the faces of the humans and their beasts were indistinguishable.

And then, right when Ash had begun to think that he'd imagined her, there she was. He'd know that striking white hair and lovely face anywhere.

She was just as beautiful as he remembered, and he decided to hate her for that, too.

He kept on the glamour he wore, the one that hid him even through the veil. Curious, he wanted to know if she could see him again; when he wasn't convinced that he'd made her up, he was sure it was solely how she seemed to look right through his glamour that caught his interest.

Only it was nearly impossible to tell. She covered her eyes with a pair of mirrored sunglasses that shielded her gaze from him. Her head was tilted downward as she fiddled with the black device she held in her hands, but Ash arrogantly followed her every move, willing her to look his way. And she did—but could she see him?

He didn't know.

And Ash hated not knowing.

She was an enigma. A riddle. A mystery he was more desperate to solve than he ever would admit.

Every shift at his guard post, he waited for her return. Since then, she hadn't missed a day. Time didn't correspond the same between worlds, and Ash only knew that his shift was over when the veil went dark. During the daylight, though, he watched and he waited and he obsessed over the female.

He tried to continue to hate her, too, but that became harder and harder as days went by.

Worse, he still didn't know if she sensed him watching or not.

When he found himself resisting the urge to walk through the veil again and confront her—something that would only incense Melisandre if he abandoned his post and she found out about it—Ash realized he needed concrete answers to his suspicions. He'd been lucky that the queen never discovered the way he crossed over the first time he spied the white-haired female, and it wasn't worth angering her again over an ordinary human.

But what if she wasn't ordinary, he wondered. What if—

There had to be some way to know for sure without drawing attention to himself.

And that's when Ash came up with it.

Kobolds.

As one of the Light Fae, Ash held dominion over some of the lower races. All he had to do was snap his finger and he could command them to do his bidding.

But while brownies were fae servants, he didn't think one of the fur-covered domestic fairies could get him the reaction he was after.

So, before he headed toward his post again, Ash created a Light Fae portal that took him from the barracks all the way to the crystal mines hidden beneath the Summer Court. In the Iron, the humans relied on their iron, their steel, their primitive technological marvels. In Faerie, magic was king—well, *queen*. While not every Light Fae was powerful enough to manage portals just like not every Dark Fae could manage shadow travel, even the weakest of his kind could use crystal to amplify their power.

And a majority of the crystal the fae harvested came from the mines controlled by the Fae Queen. Running for acres and acres beneath her crystalline palace and her favored garden, Melisandre ruled the mines with an—*ahem*—iron fist. As one of her elite guard, Ash knew exactly where its hidden entrance was located, and even though he was currently out of favor with the queen, none of his fellow soldiers stopped him as he waltzed right inside.

While his kind were in charge of guarding the mines, the actual act of mining was forced onto kobolds. Hunched, ugly, malicious creatures that came up to Ash's knee, they were master miners. Before the veil between realms closed off during the human world's industrial revolution—around the time

Oberon went missing—kobolds were considered underground spirits who could be appeased by leaving smelted gold as an offering or by showing them respect.

In Faerie, where the ruling class of the fae respected nothing and no one, they were worked as slaves, their very existence allowed at the whim of the Fae Queen.

They didn't call it the Reign of the Damned for nothing, Ash reminded himself. Melisandre often amused herself by hunting her subjects, cutting their tongues out for fun, and forcing them to sacrifice each other. Anything to keep her rule unquestioned, her power absolute. She was, of them all, completely untouchable.

And Ash didn't mean in the way he longed to touch his white-haired human, either.

Nodding at Saxon, a fellow Light Fae soldier, he used faerie fire to draw a square in the space in front of him; when he could store items in a pocket, there was never a need to fill his hands. He reached inside and pulled a burlap sack out before shaking it open.

"Which one can I take?" he asked Saxon.

A few decades younger than Ash, Saxon knew that Ash was senior both in age and in time served under the queen. With a bored expression, he just pointed at the nearest kobold, knowing better than to argue.

He didn't say thanks. It didn't even occur to Ash to

do so. He was fae, and not only would no fae ever do anything that would put them in the debt of any other being, but showing any kind of gratitude meant that he didn't have the authority to do what he wanted when he wanted.

Instead, he pinched the kobold by the back of its neck and easily dropped the suddenly still faerie into the burlap sack. The sack was enchanted to hold it until Ash set it loose again which, if everything went according to his plan, would be sooner than later.

It was risky, but what was his long, immortal life without a little risk and amusement of his own? Setting the kobold loose in the Iron was still a far better risk than chancing his queen's formidable temper again.

The way Ash saw it, either the white-haired human didn't respond to the kobold in her territory and he discovered that he imagined that she was more than just another mortal, or she *did* respond and the kobold would inevitably sense she could see it and attack her. Whatever happened, he would rid himself of this bothersome fascination.

It was worth the risk.

3

C allie avoided the park for more than a week before she realized that she was being ridiculous.

It was one thing for her to lock eyes with the golden male before quickly sliding her gaze away, as if it was just a coincidence. It was something else entirely for him to step through the veil, his intent to approach her as obvious as the layer of glamour he wore over his stunning shape.

Only it couldn't be a glamour, she told herself repeatedly. Because even when she was trying not to consciously see things, she did so anyway. Consider it more than two decades of practice or something like that. No matter how one of the faerie folk—and, from her research, she was sure she'd narrowed down his kind—glamoured themselves to appear, she always saw them as they truly were.

But that was the thing. Glamour was a lure, a way to trick unsuspecting humans close, to make them believe what they were seeing instead of hearing the clanging warning bells that said that anyone from Faerie was dangerous. If she focused, she could just about make out the image they protected, but since it often left her with a migraine, she didn't usually bother. Why, when it didn't matter?

Callie's vision showed the truth. And the truth was that, as ethereal and alluring as the fae—because fae, he had to be fae—are, the handful she'd seen always had something exaggerated about them to make them seem almost alien. From their long, slender fingers, to the eerie perfection of their features, plus their over-sized eyes... they were gorgeous, but they were also predators.

And she was tempting fate by returning to the park.

She had to, though. She managed to sell her photograph to Buster's client while also side-stepping his offer of a date. To her surprise, the older gentleman took her rejection with a smile, then actually showed some interest when she mentioned her idea of creating a summer version of the photo he bought from her.

The male fae was there upon her return, but she was prepared for it. She wore a pair of sunglasses and a floppy summer hat so even if she found it difficult not to sneak glances over at him, she was hoping he wouldn't be able to tell. And since the hours passed as she worked and he stood like a motionless statue on the other side of the veil, she figured she pulled it off.

The first round of photos were good when she developed them, but they weren't of the same caliber as the spring shot. Since part of photography relied on luck as well as skill and preparation, she had been expecting that. So, the next afternoon, she went back to the park.

And the next.

A thunderstorm rolled in, closing out the week, and while she thought about seeing how the tree would look backlit by the purple clouds and the lightning streaking across the dark sky, she remembered the charred remains of her tree and decided that maybe she should wait out the storm.

On Monday, feeling the pressure after the gentleman came to check on her progress, Callie went to the park, determined to get the shot that would get Buster's client to start talking about a possible showing again.

The first thing she noticed was that, while the shimmering patch of space that marked the veil into Faerie was still there, the fae male was not. For the handful of hours that she worked, she kept one eye on that patch. She blamed it on how careful she'd been to avoid him during her previous trips while secretly wondering where he had gone—and what had he been doing there, watching the human world, in the first place.

Then, because he wasn't there acting as her silent shadow, Callie threw herself into her work. She lost track of time as she set up, using a point and shoot digital camera to get an idea if the shot might be successful before replicating it with her professional piece. She played with angles, shutter speeds, aperture, anything to bring her vision to life.

She didn't know when he winked into sight. At first, she thought it was a stray sunbeam that blinded her before she lifted her head and saw that, instead, it was the blinding, dazzling male standing closer than he ever had before. He was still in the same spot as always, but perspective was a funny thing and Callie was a trained photographer. He was definitely closer— and he was carrying something.

She noticed all of this in a blink of her eye before she turned away, lifting her camera again, anything to keep him from noticing her in return. Ignoring him, she decided to use his shine—the only part of him that would show up in the photo as Callie knew well from experience—to highlight the tree.

So consumed with getting the perfect shot, she didn't see what happened next—but she sure as hell heard the shrieking sound that nearly blasted her poor eardrums.

Callie nearly dropped her camera. Only an ingrained instinct to never, ever drop her two thousand dollar camera had her clutching it tightly as her head jerked up in time to see a... a *thing* racing away from the hazy patch of space.

It was a dark blur, with skin the color of mahogany and a leather tunic stretched over its mis-shapened, hunched body. It loped on all fours with teeth that belonged in the mouth of a shark jutting over its jaw. Through her terror, she picked up on the glamour over-laying the creature and saw that it appeared as some kind of oversized mutt, but Callie knew better. Blinking again, she saw that it was a nightmarish creature straight out of Faerie—and *it was coming right at her*.

There wasn't even time to scream. Adrenaline coursing through her, her brain shouted at her to run while her legs stayed firmly planted on the grass as the *thing* aimed at her.

Just when she thought that this was it, right as her life was flashing before her eyes, something amazing happened—amazing because she never in a million years would've expected it to.

The golden male burst out of the veil, a brilliantly shining sword held in front of him as he arrowed after the snarling monster.

When there were barely a few feet separating Callie from the threat, the creature pounced. She braced herself, unable to do anything else, and through wide, terrified eyes she watched as the male lunged right in time to stab the length of his sword through the back of the goblin-looking thing's neck before slamming the sword—and the body—into the ground. He landed in a graceful crouch right behind his sword, his long, tawny hair rippling in the slight summer breeze.

The thing let out a garbled sound that might've been a shriek if it wasn't for the sword buried in its neck. Its four limbs twitched and jerked for a few terrible moments before it went completely still against the earth.

Callie didn't scream. She wanted to, had every intention to, and it came out as a rush of air instead.

"Holy shit," she said, the words tripping over themselves as her heart pounded wildly in her chest. "You... you saved my life."

The male had been crouched over the creature, most likely checking to see that it was dead. Which, yeah, considering it was skewered on his sword through its throat, there was a good chance it was dead. As soon as he heard Callie's strangled words, though, he slowly, gracefully rose from his crouch, pulling his sword out of the dead monster as he did.

A flash of surprise crossed his face, even more

glorious up close, but it was there and gone again by the time Callie got her frantic, frightened breathing under control.

"Yes," he said clearly, in an accented voice that was so soft, so lyrical, yet undeniably haughty. "I did."

Callie felt like she heard danger alarms going off. If there was one thing she learned from the faerie folk before she began to ignore them completely, it was pure trouble to be in their debt since they believed they were in their rights to demand anything to make things even.

And how did you make a life debt even?

She swallowed, hoping desperately that she found the one being from Faerie who saved her because he was a good samaritan.

"It came out of nowhere," she said, hoping to show him that it wasn't her fault that the toothy goblin-like creature attacked *her*. "I just saw it running with those teeth..."

The words *thank you* were on the tip of her tongue. Only the memory of a mistake in her youth—one that cost her a pint of blood, a lost baby tooth, and a promise to a sprite she hoped never got called in—kept her from saying the words. If there was any hope that he'd walk away and the two of them could go back to pretending that the other didn't exist, she had to be on her guard.

There was something about him. Something she

recognized the first time she looked in his sun-colored eyes. He wasn't anything like the faerie folk she once knew, or most of the ones she spent her teenage and young adult years avoiding.

This close, Callie could sense the power and strength humming off of him, and not only because she knew he was quick enough and forceful enough to catch up to a faerie creature and stab it like that.

"You saw it?" the male wondered. His golden eyes darkened for a heartbeat, before he resumed the same indifferent expression he'd been wearing. "So it's true, then. You're part of the *sealladh*."

Huh? "The what?"

"A human with the gift of sight. You can see me. You can see me as I am, just like you saw the kobold. Is that so?"

"Oh. I—" Callie didn't quite know how to answer him. A lie would be a mistake, and it wasn't like she could deny it when she was looking at him, talking to him, anything to keep from glancing down at the creature's body in the grass. Which, now that she thought about it, she couldn't stop herself from doing again.

She fought a shudder as she pointed and, instead of answering him, said, "Um... are you going to leave that there?"

"Does it matter? Only a human with the sight will see that it's a kobold."

Right. Because its glamour made it seem like it was

a dog. She was surprised that none of the other park goers had come by to check on her—and that's when she realized that, somehow, it had gotten much later than it had been earlier and there wasn't a single person around except for her and this male.

And he definitely wasn't a person.

She gulped. "It's still not right."

He gave her a curious look, as if he wasn't sure what to make of her. "What will you do for me?"

"Uh— what?"

"I'll remove the kobold remains, but it must be a fair trade. A bargain if you will. What will you do for me?"

Nothing.

It was just beginning to dawn on Callie that this male might be her savior, but she was already in his debt. So what if he hadn't demanded payment just yet? He would eventually.

Great.

She didn't want to get sucked in even deeper. "Forget it. If anything, animal control will come and think it's a dog."

"That's not necessary. I'll do it for your name."

"My name?"

It was a question. A way to verify that that was all he wanted from her. But no matter how she meant it, it didn't matter if the fae could use her words against her. As if he hadn't heard the questioning lilt, he clearly took it as if she was offering her name since he swept down and, spearing the kobold's crumpled body with his sword again, he easily hefted up the corpse, dropping it into the burlap sack he had tied at his hip.

It must be magic, she thought, watching as the bag swallowed up the three-foot high creature before shrinking to a much smaller size.

The fae male did something then. Cupping his right hand, he conjured something that looked like a fireball. Then, drawing with the pointer finger on his left hand, he traced a small square. Wherever his finger went, a flame leapt to take its place until Callie was looking at a fiery shape floating between them. He pushed the bag with the monster's body up against it and, in an instant, it was gone.

He waved his now empty hands. The fire extinguished with a faint *pop*, leaving only a trail of a barely there wisp of pale smoke.

"There," he said. "Now tell me your name, human."

In the back of her mind, Callie bristled. She knew he was different—that he was *other*—and there was no denying the layer of disdain oozing off of his clear voice when he called her *human* like that. She wanted to refuse him. To shake her head and, clutching her camera, just dash away from the park.

He wouldn't follow her, would he? There was no reason he would unless he intended to call in her debt for saving her right then.

One look at the determination blazing in his fiery gaze, though, and Callie had her answer.

He would. He definitely would.

This magnificent male stepped out of his world to save her. Even if he regarded her as one of the primitive humans who lived on the other side of the veil, he shielded her from the toothy, snarling creature, and he had gotten rid of its remains.

"Callie," she offered. "My name is Callie."

"Take me to your home, Callie."

No, screamed her sense of self-preservation.

"Okay," she breathed out.

HIS NAME WAS ASH. At least, that's what he told her to call him during the short walk back to Callie's apartment.

He offered to whip up a portal, whatever that meant, but while she was still grateful for his save, she wasn't so enchanted that she was going to follow a creature of Faerie into some kind of "portal". She'd read the stories. She'd done her research. If she wasn't careful, she could end up trapped in Faerie.

No, thanks.

She also knew she couldn't just refuse him. Ever since she first locked eyes with the golden male, she'd thumbed through all of her books, hoping that her instincts were wrong. She was convinced that he was Seelie, one of the Light Fae, and a member of the ruling class in Faerie. Referred to as the Blessed Ones, that was only when you compared them to their dark counterparts, the Unseelie.

Whether they were called Dark or Light, though, fae were fae. It would be a mistake to offend him, just like she knew better than to give him her full name or follow him anywhere. It probably wasn't the smartest idea to show him where she lived, either, but she couldn't figure out how to get rid of him without insulting him.

When they arrived at her building, she hesitated before walking inside. At this time of day, Mitch would be at work, but she still had her neighbors to worry about. Since she'd lived there, she'd never brought anyone home with her, especially not such a stunning creature. From the faint haze surrounding him, she knew he was using glamour so she could only imagine how much more attractive he looked, if that was even possible.

It had to be, Callie decided. Despite her nerves and her instincts kicking her for getting involved with this Ash, she hadn't been too distracted not to notice all of the women—and some men—breaking their necks to get a better look at him as he all but swept gracefully at her side. He caught the attention of almost everyone they passed, but the strangest thing was that he was focused solely on her.

That should've been her first clue that something wasn't quite right.

Callie got lucky. The doorman's post was empty, and she didn't run into any of her neighbors as she crossed the lobby, heading right for the elevator.

She jammed the "up" button with her thumb, too unsettled to make small talk with her new shadow as they waited for the car to return to the first floor. When it did, Callie stepped inside, then waited for Ash.

The fae moved to follow her but one step over the threshold and he froze. His eyes seemed to flash beneath the fluorescent bulbs as he glanced around the cramped space before he shot out his hand, stopping the doors from shutting them inside of the elevator. Callie could've sworn she heard something sizzle, but the sound only lasted a second before Ash moved out of the elevator and back into the lobby.

Maybe it was the dim lighting out there, but it seemed as if he lost some of his deeply bronzed color.

The arrogant expression, though?

Yeah, she decided as she slipped out of the elevator after him, that wasn't going anywhere.

"Is there another way to your home?" he asked. "Without using that box? There must be stairs."

"Um. Yeah. I live on the tenth floor, though."

He arched an eyebrow. From the cut of his uniform

to the corded forearm peeking out from under the loose sleeve, Callie was willing to bet that ten flights would be nothing for someone like him—and that wasn't even taking in account that he was from a magical other realm. While she usually would get winded after three, he could probably take the ten flights and still be good for another ten.

"Okay," she said. "If you insist."

There was that spark in his gaze again. She couldn't tell if it was interest or, most likely, scrutiny. That she was something he didn't understand, and that he was working toward figuring her out.

So it was no surprise to her at all when he said, "Oh. I do insist."

Callie fought the shiver running down her spine. This was a bad idea, she knew. A very bad idea. She wasn't even sure why she was entertaining it. The shock over the toothy goblin-like creature might've gotten him this far, but now that she was safe at home, it would be the very height of stupidity to invite further danger into her personal space, especially with Mitch out.

And yet—

"Come on."

4

She was right about his stamina. While she was discreetly trying to hide her huffing and puffing, Ash didn't even seem to notice the upward climb to her floor. His long legs ate up the steps, with Callie struggling to stay ahead of him. Eventually she just let him go since, if he passed the tenth floor, it would be his fault for not paying attention.

She found him waiting beneath the large number "10" sign hanging over the exit. With a sheepish shrug, she scooted by him, leading him toward her apartment.

Still he followed.

In front of her apartment, she dug around her purse, searching for her keys. She grabbed them, then quickly opened the door before one of her neighbors popped their head out to say 'hi'.

Once inside, she set her camera bag and her purse down on the nearest flat space, waiting for his reaction. When he didn't say anything, she followed his gaze, seeing the shabby furniture and the scattered mess in a whole new light. It was all she and Mitch could afford when they pooled their resources after they moved in together after graduation and, well, if it ain't broke, right?

Still, she sent a glance over at Ash as he ran his eyes over the living room. He was the first otherworldly being she'd ever allowed into her space.

Sue her for being a little nervous.

"You live in an iron cage," he said at last.

"Oh. Um. Well, yeah. I guess I do." She darted around the room, clearing up some clutter and garbage, using a decorative couch pillow to cover up the laundry she meant—and forgot—to fold last night. "It's kind of all I can afford. City prices, you know? And I even have to share it with my roomie."

"Someone else lives here?"

Callie nodded. "Mitch. He should be home in a bit if you want to meet him. Not that I'm asking you to. I mean, we just met. But... just so you know. He usually gets home by eight."

"After the shadows come?"

Did he mean night? "I think so."

"I'll be gone by then."

"Sure. Yeah. Of course."

Ash moved toward her, closing the space between the two of them. She was holding a stack of empty paper plates, some crumpled napkins, and a half-filled can of Diet Coke. Without really knowing why, she gulped, then turned away and darted into the kitchen. Callie hurriedly placed it all on top of the tiny, crooked table placed up against the wall.

He moved gracefully into the cramped space, blocking her from her next escape.

"Tell me about this Mitch."

Her hands clear again, she wiped them nervously on her jeans. "What do you want to know?"

"Is he your *ffrindau*?" Ash asked, emphasizing the last word.

"My friend?" she clarified. "Yeah. We grew up in the same neighborhood together. When neither of us could afford to move out on our own, we decided to split this place after we finished school. It's alright. Small," she admitted, thinking about the way he called her space a cage, "but it's better than nothing. And we get along pretty well."

Ash took a step into her, cocking his head slightly as he studied her closely again. His long, tawny hair shifted, settling over his lean shoulder. He frowned for a heartbeat before his expression settled into that haughty glare she was beginning to think of as his default.

"Is he your mate?"

"Mate?" she echoed. "Yeah. I told you. He's my friend."

"Not friend," corrected Ash. "Mate. The one you allow to touch you. The one you take into your bed. A lover?"

Callie nearly choked. "God, no. Why would you ask that?"

He didn't answer her.

"He's just my roommate," she said again. "He has his room. I have mine. We share the kitchen and the living room. That's all."

Ash pursed his lips, then said the last thing she expected from a fae she'd just met: "Tell him not to return."

"What?"

"The other male. *Mitch*. If I'll be coming to see you in this place, I want him gone. The iron is bad enough. But another male? I won't tolerate it."

Callie blinked. Okay. The scrutiny was one thing. Walking her home to her apartment after her scare in the park, that was a nicety she wouldn't expect from one of his kind. Then again, maybe it *wasn't* a nicety.

Somewhere along the way, signals had been majorly crossed. She had to fix them and *now*.

"I'm sorry, but... you're fae, right?"

He didn't seem surprised that she knew. In fact, his sun-colored eyes brightened in... pride? Huh. It almost seemed like he was proud that she could tell.

"Yes," he told her. "I am one of the Blessed Ones. A Light Fae who serves the Seelie Court."

So she was right. Score one for her research books.

"Like I said. Fae. Okay. Are all fae nuts? You're the first I ever talked to—the first who actually treated me like a person instead of a curiosity—so I'm not sure. But... and I'm not trying to offend you or anything... but that's nuts. I can't kick Mitch out for a faerie creature I just met."

Though Ash's golden eyes seemed to blaze with some fierce emotion when she called him a "faerie creature", he didn't erupt like she almost expected him to. Instead, he quirked his lips in a mockery of a charming smile.

"You can, Callie," he said cajolingly. "You will."

"Um. No."

"No?"

"No."

Something happened. She couldn't understand it —didn't know how to explain it—but she *felt* it. A pulse of electricity, a sudden surge, and every single bulb in the kitchen simply exploded.

Pop! Pop! Pop! Pop!

Callie shrieked, covering her head at the first *pop*-ping sound. Her first wild thought was *it's gunshots* and she desperately tried to shield herself as she threw herself to the ground. Glass shattered, hitting the hard-wood floor around her.

After a moment, she dared a peek up. Ash was standing in front of her, twinkling dust glittering in his long hair. He gave it a royal shake, knocking some of the shards to the floor.

What the—

She looked higher. And that's when she noticed that the four light bulbs screwed into the ceiling fan over Ash's head had blown out.

Scrambling to her knees, she snapped, "What the hell just happened?"

"Don't worry about that. Now come here."

She was right. She was so, so right. The fae was nuts *and she invited him into her home*.

She knew better than to do that. Twenty years of seeing creatures from Faerie—twenty years of pretending she couldn't—and she lost her head over the first pretty one who paid her any attention. If it wasn't for the fact that her gift meant she was basically immune to their charm and their compulsion spells, she would've thought that Ash had glamoured her, tricked her into taking him home with her.

But no. That bit of brilliance had been all Callie.

When she stayed where she was, Ash held out his hand. "Callie. Come."

Seriously? Slowly, Callie stood, something warning her against touching him even as she just resisted the urge to shove him out of her apartment.

That haughty expression of his was really starting to piss her off.

"Do you think I'm a dog?" she demanded, glass crackling under her sneaker as she firmly planted her foot. "Because I'm not just going to come when I'm called."

For all his looming and his arrogance, she had a hunch that the most he would do was bully her to get his way. He'd never *force* her. So, hoping she was right, she stayed right where she was.

There was that frown again. If she didn't know better—if she thought a fae male could be vulnerable enough to let her see any kind of weakness—she would've thought he looked confused.

Or maybe he forgot that he was dealing with— what did he call it? Someone with the "gift of sight".

She could see him as his eyebrows drew in; if he wasn't such an ethereal beauty, she was sure his forehead would've wrinkled, too. His lush lips parted before his eyes widened in sudden understanding.

"Callie is not your true name."

That was the last thing she expected him to say.

"You're talking about my real name? No. It's not. It's a nickname."

"Did you mean to deceive me on purpose?"

"By telling you that I'm Callie?" She shook her head. "It's my name. You didn't need to know what's on my birth certificate."

Especially since this wasn't Callie's first run-in with a faerie creature sneaking around the human world, sure that their glamour would fool her. She might not know many of their secrets—and that was on purpose, too, since she was a profound believer that ignorance could be bliss—but she knew very well that giving one of the fae her true name was one way to give them power over her.

"Tell me. Tell me what you're really called."

He had to be kidding.

"No."

Ash was quick. With a glide so graceful it belonged on a stage, he crossed the lingering space between them, his hands hovering over her upper arms. She could sense him, but he didn't quite make contact with her skin, and she wasn't so sure why that was an overwhelming relief, but it was.

His face only inches from hers as she jerked her head back, he cooed, "You *will* tell me."

This was getting to be too much. She might've had her own moment of temporary insanity when she invited this capricious creature into her home, but that was easily corrected. The same gut instinct from before whispered that he would bully and he would push until she stood up for herself. Only then would this magnificent male back off.

She swallowed and, shuffling a few steps away from him, she stubbornly said, "No. I won't."

"You refuse me?"

There was something in the way he said *refuse* that had Callie choosing her next words carefully. "I think you should go."

"I have plenty of time until the sun sets and I have to return to Faerie. You invited me in. I'm not going anywhere."

Oh? Was he so sure of that?

Remembering the way he stepped into the elevator and quickly moved back out again, the sizzling sound as his hand made contact with the metal door, and how he commented with a faint sneer that her apartment was a cage of iron, Callie slowly moved back and away from Ash. Iron... how could she have forgotten the fae's disdain for iron?

He followed her with his unblinking gaze, but he didn't make another move. Good. That gave Callie time to make a break for it and lunge for the kitchen countertop—the countertop and Mitch's favored cast iron pan resting on top of it. He always swore it made his steaks taste better than any of her cheap set of cookware, and because it was so big and so heavy, he just kept it stored by the stove.

For the first time ever, Callie didn't give a shit that it was an eyesore.

It was heavier than she remembered, but she was panicking a little at the way he watched her like a spider sizing up the poor fly caught in its web. Weight didn't mean a damn thing as she used two hands to grab the handle, swinging the cast iron pan up like it was a baseball bat and she was Mark McGwire.

"Back up," she warned Ash. "Back up or I'll use this. I swear I will."

One glimpse at the murderous expression that flitted across his flawless features told Callie that she was right. Ash wouldn't push her while she was wielding the pan, but he definitely wasn't happy about that.

Like before, though, he wrangled his expression quickly. He obviously wasn't used to dealing with a human he couldn't control. Her gift—her sight—made them more evenly matched since Callie knew to be on her guard. He got under her skin once. She wasn't so sure what this fae would do if she let him do it again.

And he proved it a moment later when he scoffed and said, "You won't escape me that easily, Callie."

"Are you threatening me?" A waver slipped into her tone. So much for being brave, but the look on the fae's face... it would bring even the strongest human to their knees. Were her instincts wrong? On a shaky breath, she demanded to know, "Are you going to hurt me?"

Ash stayed silent for a moment before he asked, "Why would I?"

Good question.

Callie hefted the cast iron pan as high as she possibly could. She didn't know him. She didn't really know what he was, what he was capable of. He was fae, but what exactly did that mean?

One thing she did know? From the way he glared at the iron pan, she was convinced that it was probably the only thing keeping him away from her at that very moment.

For some strange reason, he seemed to be fixated on her; wrangling an invitation after he crossed into her world and skewered the kobold was one thing, but the way he tried to order her to kick Mitch out proved that to Callie's mind. And, sure, he *had* saved her from that *thing* ... but that didn't mean she was going to let him walk all over her just because he was powerful enough to do so—and cocky enough to think that she would let him.

She swallowed, and though her arms were killing her, she held on tightly to the pan. "Goodbye, Ash."

"You're daring," he said. "I'll give you that. But you're making this more difficult than it has to be. You've caught my attention, human. For good or for bad, you have it."

"What if I don't want it?"

A small quirk of his lush lips. "You should've thought about that before you invited me home."

And then, before she could retort, Ash walked out of the kitchen without another word.

Callie didn't lower the heavy pan—or take another

breath—until she heard the front door open, then close.

Though she knew she was probably making a huge mistake, she lugged the cast iron pan out of the kitchen, down the hall, and over to the door. She wasn't brave enough to open it in case Ash took it as another invitation, but she peered out through the peephole.

Then, in shock at what she saw, she fumbled with the knob before throwing her shoulder into the wood, swinging the door wide just in time to watch the last of the tower of flames dissipate.

Because that's what she had seen. A wall of fire that stretched from the ceiling to the industrial carpet. Ash's mysterious portal? It had to be, especially since there was no sign that it had been there except for the heat licking out at her and the scent of flowers that filled the normally musty hall.

No scorch marks.

No smoke.

No Ash.

He was gone, but Callie's instincts told her that he wouldn't be for long.

5

S he was just sweeping up the last of the glass when Mitch let himself into the apartment.

Thinking ahead, Callie changed out the lightbulbs before she started cleaning. She could explain away the glass shards way more easily than she could a dark kitchen so she looted the under the sink area for as many spare bulbs as she could find first, then reached for the broom second.

While she cleaned, she had some time to think. As grateful as she was that the fae male—that Ash—had crossed over to save her from the fierce faerie creature heading for her, it all seemed so very coincidental now that he was gone and she could think more clearly. He might not be able to use his glamour to trick her into believing everything he said, but his natural, glamour-free form was still so dazzling that Callie had definitely fallen under his sway a bit. Why else would she have brought him to her home? He wasn't a vampire, so it wasn't like he needed the invitation, but when it came to entering into bargains and contracts and agreements with the faerie folk—whether she meant to or not— she had to be careful not to give him so much an inch otherwise he'd take a mile.

It was bad enough that his rescue came with an unknown price tag. After the way she had to all but chase him off with her roommate's cast iron pan, Callie was beginning to have serious doubts that she could pay it.

Not that she could tell Mitch any of that. By the time she heard the door opening and, peeking into the hall, saw that it was her roommate, she had pulled on her own version of glamour. The last thing she needed was Mitch letting slip to her family that she was "having trouble" again.

Twenty-two or not, her parents would insist on more therapy—and that was if they didn't guilt her into moving back home, too. Callie would rather deal with the fae on her own than have her parents think she was struggling.

So, quickly sweeping the last of the broken glass into the dustpan before dumping it in the trash, Callie offered Mitch a welcoming smile as he tossed his messenger bag on top of the couch.

Mitch was the same age as Callie, and she might

have downplayed her relationship with him just a bit when Ash asked her about it. While it had never been a romantic one, mainly because it seemed weird to her to be into her brother-in-law's brother, Callie considered Mitch her closest friend. He knew about her history with "seeing things" and had never treated her any differently for it, even if she knew her mother and her sister quizzed him about her whenever they got a chance.

And that was when they weren't already playing matchmaker, convinced that Mitch and Callie were meant to be together.

He was good-looking in his own way, she admitted. He had shaggy dark blond hair that was perpetually in need of a haircut, and his tall, lanky body always seemed a little too big whenever his office required him to wear a suit. Most days, though, a polo and jeans were fine, and that's what he was wearing now.

"Good day at work?" she asked him.

He groaned, rolling his head on his neck. His shoulders looked tight, and he lifted a hand to rub away at the obvious tension.

"Long day, Cal," he said. "And I got a longer one tomorrow. Gotta be up at the crack of dawn for a whole slate of meetings. I was thinking about ordering in, then heading right to sleep. You hungry?"

Huh. With everything that happened, Callie hadn't had anything to eat since her early lunch. Glancing out the kitchen window, she saw that it was dark. It must've been more than seven hours since her last meal and, now that Mitch mentioned it, she realized she was *starving*.

"I can eat."

"Pizza?"

"You buy, I tip tonight?"

While they usually cooked for themselves, on the rare occasion that they spent money on a meal out, they were on a rotating system. Callie got the last round of take-out for them so it was Mitch's turn.

"Sounds good. Pepperoni on your half?"

She nodded. "Get some garlic knots, too. Okay?"

Mitch nodded, pulling out his expensive Nokia cellphone. Callie hadn't bothered getting a cell—partly because of the price, and partly because she'd never get her parents off her back if they could contact her at any given moment—but Mitch's job provided him with his. He was kind of pretentious with it, but at least when he wasn't using it he let Callie play "Snake", so it wasn't *so* annoying.

"I'll place the order, then hop in the shower. Here." He reached into his front pocket, pulled out a twenty, and offered it to Callie. "In case I'm still getting ready. Nunzio's is usually pretty quick."

She accepted it, making a mental note to grab a couple of singles from her purse to give him as change since twenty was more than enough for food and tip.

"No problem. Take your time in there," she said, a teasing note finding its way to her voice. "You look like you need to relax a little."

Mitch didn't even try to deny it. With a shrug, he said, "It's what happens when I live with a babe who doesn't want to be friends with benefits."

In response to his obvious innuendo, Callie stuck out her tongue.

Mitch pointed at her. "Hey. Don't stick it out unless you want to use it."

"You wish."

"I do, Cal. I really do."

She rolled her eyes. Their relationship was built on mutual affection, but despite his teasing and his flirting, she knew that he only made comments like that because *he* knew she wouldn't take any offense to it. Of course, if she offered to join him in the shower, he'd never say no, but it wasn't like he was carrying a torch for her or anything and they both knew *that*.

Mitch chuckled at her reaction before waving his phone at her, then heading down the hall toward the bathroom.

"Don't forget my pepperoni," she called after him.

"I won't," he promised as he went inside to start the shower.

A few minutes later, Callie heard the water come on, then the bathroom door open again. As she set the broom to the side, she waited to see if he would call out to her. Maybe the pizzeria was out of pepperoni or something—

A towel draped around his naked waist, Mitch's bare feet slapped against the hallway floor. Callie held her breath, hoping none of the glass made its way out of the kitchen, as her roommate padded past her, toward the front door.

"Mitch, I don't think the pizza could've gotten here yet."

"Not the pizza," came his reply. She heard him mutter a couple of words under his breath, the sound of something sliding across something else, and then, "Cal, did you see my watch?"

"What?"

"My watch. I forgot to grab it this morning, and I just remembered when I went to take it off for the shower. I'm pretty sure I left it over here on this table, but it's gone."

She joined him by their front door.

Mitch was standing next to the same side table near the couch where she'd dropped her purse and her camera bag. There were usually a few other knick-knacks scattered along the top—a remote, an extra scrunchie, a pair of sunglasses—and she tried to remember if Mitch's watch had been there earlier.

If it had been, it wasn't now.

Oh, no.

No, no, no.

Callie had a bad feeling about that.

Her purse was shoved to the side, the mouth of it open. Her camera bag was resting precariously on the edge of the table. She didn't know if Mitch had moved it during his search, or if a sticky-fingered fae might have had a chance to go through their things on his way out of the apartment.

It had seemed like forever before he actually left. But would a magical, otherworldly being snatch Mitch's Timex watch, so cheap that it wasn't even waterproof?

More importantly, if she dug through her purse, would anything of hers be missing?

Her heart started beating triple-time again. She didn't know for sure, but she'd learned a long time ago to trust her senses—her instincts, her hearing, her sight—over anything else.

And her senses were telling her she had a pretty good idea where Mitch's watch had gone.

Even so, she shrugged, and then she answered him while hoping like hell it wasn't a lie.

"Nope. Never saw it."

IN HIS BARRACKS ONCE MORE, Ash went to his private quarters and, pressing his thumb to the crystal knob he'd imprinted on once he made Melisandre's elite guard, he locked himself inside.

Up until that instant, he refused to allow himself to focus on the events of what happened in the Iron. Dwelling too closely on it would've ignited in Ash the desire to compel his white-haired human—his Callie —to come with him, to talk to him, to even tell him no repeatedly as she refused him if only because he was sure he'd get her to change her mind eventually.

But he had also felt the pull of the shadows and he knew that it wasn't worth fighting the darkness when his time with the human was only beginning. She'd had a fright that, he admitted, he was solely responsible for, and now that he had proved that she had the sight, he had to be far more careful in how he approached her.

Because never seeing her again was *not* an option.

The moment he let the kobold loose, directing it to run through the veil and cross over into the human world, Ash had just wanted to know what it was about her that kept him coming back. Sure, Melisandre's command had him at the post, but he didn't try to convince her otherwise because he wanted to go. Because he was interested in a human. There was no denying that.

Just like how there was no denying the way his protective instincts came roaring to life as soon as the kobold took off after her.

Nothing could have stopped him from going after the creature. It didn't matter that he was the one who sent it running toward Callie. From the terror that slammed into her like a wave, reaching out to him even through the veil, to the way she stared at the kobold without trying to escape it, Ash had his answer. She could see it—she could see *him*—and, suddenly, he wanted to hold onto his fascination with her.

His human female needed to live so the kobold had to die. He wasn't even thinking about what it would mean to save her life until she, still stunned, pointed out that he had. And, with just those words, she unknowingly triggered a geas similar to that of Nine's.

Ash was protective of his human, but he was still fae. He would use that life debt to get what he wanted, no matter what.

Once locked inside his personal quarters, Ash reached into the deep pockets of his pants, pulling out the contents inside. When he could store everything he could or would ever need in a faerie portal, the things he kept on his person were the most important things he owned.

Normally there was only one thing in his pants. Today, there were three.

Nestled in the crook of his bronzed palm, he saw his pebble. A symbol of the life debt that Ninetroir owed him, Ash never went without it; the geas would still exist even if he lost the small rock, but he liked knowing he had visible evidence of it. Nine was a Dark Fae, one of the Cursed Ones. He was much younger than Ash, and he'd recently joined the queen's guard after completing the academy at Ash's request, but they weren't friends.

The fae didn't have friends.

They did, however, have a fated mate. Known as their *ffrindau*, each of the fae was promised a soulmate, though so many of his kind didn't put much stock in the fanciful notion. They took mates as they pleased while acknowledging that any union would only last until a *ffrindau* came and shattered it.

Ash had never thought he'd find his. Born more than three centuries ago, he wasn't as young as Nine, but he was still considered a youth to his kind. Most fae didn't find their *ffrindau* until they measured their years in millennia instead of centuries, and since he had never lacked for female companionship, his fated mate was an idea instead of a reality.

It still was, but after how his every instinct told him to save Callie from the kobold, he wasn't so sure anymore.

And, for one of the fae, being unsure was very, very dangerous.

Next to the pebble, he looked at the watch that had stopped ticking as soon as he brought it through the portal and into Faerie. A soldier through and through, Ash was always thinking ahead. He'd grabbed the timepiece before he left Callie's cage, sensing from its aura that it belonged to the male who had imprinted on her home.

The *Mitch* she spoke of.

Ash wasn't so certain he would need it, but it never hurt to be prepared. He wanted to believe that mindset led him to also take the third item he was holding, but Ash knew better.

He took Callie's tiny hairbrush because he wanted to bring something of hers with him, and he was pleased that it held countless strands of her lovely, pale hair.

Using two long, slender fingers, he unthreaded a single strand, holding it up to his eyes in open inspection. It wasn't quite white, he decided, but more of a white-blonde. There was a distinction, and it had everything to do with his curious human.

So engrossed in deciphering its shade, Ash never realized that he had company until it was too late.

A knock sounded at his door. "Open up, soldier."

Ash disappeared the pebble, the watch, the brush full of her lovely white-blonde hair back into his pocket. He patted the bulge along his hip, making his uniform as pristine as possible, then pressed his thumb to the crystal again.

The lock disengaged with a soft *snick*. Before Ash could reach to grip the knob, it was already turning.

The door swung outward, revealing a Light Fae with an extra row of golden buttons along his collar.

Captain Helix.

"Evening, Captain."

Helix nodded at Ash. "I've come because of the queen."

Of course he had. Helix was the captain of her guard, and though rumors among the ranks wondered how much longer he would keep the post when his loyalty was tied much closer to the throne than to who sat on it, he had managed to do something most deemed impossible: he'd kept his head these last two centuries.

A formidable male, and one that managed a second impossible feat: he had earned Ash's respect during the last of the Shadow Wars.

The Shadows Wars—fought between the Dark Fae who refused to accept that the Fae Queen was also their ruler, and the Light Fae who enforced Melisandre's whim—had ended more than a century ago. Before she became queen, the Summer King ruled the Seelie Court while the Winter Queen ruled over the Unseelie Court, including the Shadow Realm. Despite how sick the Shadow Realm made the Light Fae soldiers, they still succeeded with the help of the Wild Hunt, driving the Dark Fae soldiers further into the shadows.

If it wasn't for the fact that, shortly after Oberon

disappeared, the Winter Queen also vanished, maybe the Dark Fae would have had a better chance. But with both monarchs lost, Melisandre found it all too easy to take control of their thrones.

There were still too many casualties during the wars, too many immortal lives cut down. While some of the lesser faerie races could be dispatched more easily than others—including kobolds—a fae could survive any wound save for decapitation. There were other fae-killers, too, of course. A Brinkburn, banishment to the Iron, too many shadows for the Seelie, sunlight to the Dark Fae... but when it came to mortal wounds, chopping off a fae's head was the only way to go.

None were faster with a sword than Helix, Ash recalled. He struck down their enemies without hesitation, but he wasn't a merciless killer. Those who didn't deserve death kept their heads and, deep down, Ash respected that.

Which was why, though his hand itched to grab his own sword, he steadied it. Before he jumped to the conclusion that Melisandre had learned of his trip into the Iron, he might as well find out why Helix was actually there.

"What is it the queen wants from me?"

"There's a skirmish in Scáth," Helix explained. Scáth was the largest city in the Winter Court, and a site of more than a few battles during the last war.

"The queen has sent a few guards to shut it down before it becomes trouble."

That would explain why there had been no whisper of Nine and his shadows lurking around the barracks lately. A formidable shade-walker, Melisandre would've sent the Dark Fae to control some of his more restless brethren.

As a Light Fae, Ash couldn't create a portal in the Unseelie Court. He'd have to go by horse if he was needed to join the other soldiers, and that meant a journey through the Shadow Realm. The dense shadow would drain Ash almost as effectively as the Iron did, but he would do it because it was his duty, even if Melisandre would surely just think of it as another way to punish him.

And it would be a punishment, but not in the way the queen would hope for. Ash was a formidable soldier who'd survived long tours in the harsh Winter lands of Faerie. A quick jaunt to Scáth to stifle any new rebellions would be nothing to him—but leaving the puzzle of his white-haired human behind for longer than he cared to?

Ash's gut twisted in some unfamiliar emotion. Layering on his glamour—unlike Callie, Helix would only see what Ash wanted him to see—he used the shield to hide his sudden discomfort.

Then, in as unconcerned a voice as he could

manage, he asked, "Does she want me to go? Is that why she's sent you here?"

"No."

Ash narrowed his gaze on the captain. "Then what does she want?"

Helix gave a graceful shrug of his shoulders, his layer of glamour just as thick as Ash's, if not thicker.

What was the good captain hiding, Ash wondered?

And then Helix said, "Melisandre wants nothing from you which, considering she's still furious you caught her with her glamour down, is a very good thing. Still, I speak for her."

Ash's suspicion only rose. "I'm still waiting to understand, Captain."

"It's very simple. The palace guard is not as strong with some of our best on the frontlines, and it's foolish to have an elite soldier wasting his time on the edge of the realm when he could be better used elsewhere. I can make that happen for you, Aislinn. Just say the word."

Helix had his name, but since Ash hadn't gifted it to him, the captain couldn't use it to command or compel him. Still, it was a reminder of who Ash was, who Helix was, and how fickle the creature they both served could be.

Melisandre used her subjects' true names as a warning. What about Helix? What would he want in return for his "help"? Changing his post from the edge of Faerie to the Fae Queen's crystal palace wasn't a favor exactly, or even a bargain, but it was enough to tilt the scales toward the captain if Ash accepted.

Good thing he had no intention of doing so—and not just because he loathed the idea of being in anyone's debt.

"Don't intercede on my behalf. I'm fine where I am."

Helix nodded. "If you change your mind, let me know. I'll talk to the queen."

Ash thought of the brush in his pocket, and his plan to cross back into the Iron as soon as he possibly could.

"As you say, Captain."

6

Knock, knock.
    Knock, knock.
    Knock, knock, knock...

Callie groaned. She had the very tempting desire to pick up her pillow, cover her head with it, and pretend like she couldn't hear the constant rapping coming from her front door.

It was a brisk knock with a bit of force behind it. Not quite a banging, but tell that to the pounding of her skull as it beat in rhythm to it.

Quirking open an eye, she peered at her alarm clock. It hadn't gone off yet, so she knew she wasn't late, and when she saw that it said seven, she scowled. It was one of her two off days, and while Callie was a morning person, she did like to sleep in until at least eight or nine when she didn't have to be at Buster's by six.

Who the hell was knocking at her door at seven in the morning?

Throwing her blanket away from her, she got up. If she could hear the rapping all the way in her bedroom, then so could her neighbors. One of the downsides of apartment living. Unless she wanted the Johanssons giving her the stink eye or Mrs. Moseley stopping over later to bitch, she might as well take care of this now that her headache made it impossible to go back to sleep.

It had to be her, Callie remembered. Last night over pizza, Mitch had gone into detail about the big meetings he had set-up for that morning. They were a huge deal and he was pretty nervous over them.

Mitch really was working hard toward that promotion of his, promising her that he'd be around a lot more once he got it. For now, his hours were long, he often took work home with him, and even though it was seven, he had to have left the apartment already.

As she shuffled toward the door, she thought she might've figured out who was out there. Despite her suspicions when it came to the fae male, she couldn't *quite* blame Mitch's missing watch on Ash when her roommate had a bad habit of misplacing his things pretty frequently.

How much did she want to bet that he came back to the apartment because he lost something else?

As she reached for the doorknob, she called out, "Mitch? What's up?" She swung the door in. "Did you forget your key or something—"

Not Mitch. It wasn't Mitch.

And Callie reeeeaally should've looked through the peephole first.

Before she could slam the door in his face, Ash swept into the apartment as if he had every right to be there.

Once he was standing in the middle of the living room, he spun on his heel, the same arrogant expression back on his handsome face as he took the entirety of her apartment in.

Mitch wasn't there. It was a good thing, too, because as much as she had believed that she hadn't seen the last of Ash yesterday, she'd never expected him to show up early the next morning.

And what it hadn't been her day off? On a normal morning, Callie would've already been at Buster's while Mitch would've been having a morning cup of coffee before heading into his office at nine. How the hell would she have explained his appearance at the apartment then? Sure, Ash was layered in a thick glamour while he stalked around the human world, but still. Mitch would have questions.

Shit, *she* had questions.

"What are you—"

Ash cut her off with a clicking of his tongue. Finishing his quick perusal, Ash turned her way, looking down his perfect, perfect nose at her. "You didn't get rid of the other male, Callie."

Pop!

She sighed as the light bulb in the living room lamp exploded. This time, she didn't duck. It was only the one, and she was beginning to guess what was causing it.

So, instead of being scared, she just got annoyed.

"Can you stop destroying my apartment? That was the last bulb I had, you know."

"Then you should've done as I told you. I don't want him here with you."

"That's funny. Because I don't want you here with me, either."

The corner of his mouth lifted. Callie didn't know what it was that she said or did to get that sort of reaction out of him, but maybe her approach was working. After all of the thinking she did while she was sweeping up the kitchen last night, she had come up with a kind of game plan in case Ash *did* return. Acting as if she couldn't be bothered by his presence was right there at the top.

He was fae. A cocky, smug, pretentious being who thought he could tell her what to do if only because he was fae and she was human. If she let him steamroll over her, she'd only prove him right. She had no idea why he demanded an invitation to her home yesterday —just like she didn't understand why he was back— but she figured that, if she made every moment with her difficult, he'd get the hint and fixate on another human.

And, if she was lucky, he'd forget all about how he saved her and how, to one of the faerie folk, that meant something.

Callie wasn't from Faerie. She didn't have to abide by their ancient traditions or their set of laws so twisted, even a lawyer would find it difficult to keep them straight.

And if she kept telling herself that, maybe she'd believe it.

"What are you doing here?" she demanded, finally remembering to close the front door before she stalked toward him.

"Did I wake you?" His eyes took in her sleep-tousled hair, the probable crease from the pillowcase across her cheek, and her disheveled nightshirt. His burning gaze dipped from top to bottom, head to toe, lingering on her bare thighs before locking on her chest. He spoke to her tits when he murmured softly, "I waited until well after sunrise to return."

Callie followed his stare. Crap. It was bad enough that the shirt she slept in last night barely fell past her ass, but the material was worn and thin. While that made it super comfortable as a nightshirt, she just remembered that the white was nearly see-through—and she never slept in a bra.

"I asked you what you're doing here," she said again, barely resisting the urge to cross her arms over her chest. And then, when all he did was continue to keep up with that heated stare, she said, "And I don't just mean my apartment. The park. Yesterday. What do you want with me?"

He quirked one immaculately shaped eyebrow. "Haven't you figured that out yet?"

Ash had the most beautiful voice. She assumed it was another tool in his arsenal, another lure. When even the timbre of his voice had goosebumps sprouting along her arms, Callie was finding it harder and harder to stay unaffected.

Haven't you figured that out yet?

Welp, she hadn't. Not really. At least, not last night.

But now, with Ash standing like a shining beacon in her drab city apartment, too dazzling to be real even though her sight said he was, Callie had to admit she had an inkling of an idea. She might only be twenty-two, and she could only guess how old an immortal creature of Faerie might be, but she'd been an early bloomer. Since she was a young teen, she'd gotten used to older men—and she was pretty sure Ash *definitely* qualified as an older man—seeing right through any clothes she was wearing, basically fucking her with their eyes.

Just like Ash was doing right now. His sun-colored eyes had darkened slightly, turning to a shade like molten gold; she could just about feel the heat stretching in the space between them.

He wanted her.

Why?

No clue.

Was it possible?

Callie wouldn't have guessed since, despite twenty-two years of the sight, none of the other faerie creatures had ever looked at her as anything other than a curiosity—or, on a few terrifying occasions, a *snack*.

And, oh, Ash looked like he wanted to gobble her up just then, but not in the way some of the creatures like that kobold had.

Flustered. Callie was suddenly flustered. Figuring it was too late to hide out in her room or run and grab a robe or something, she decided to own her sleeping attire at the same time as she pointedly ignored his blatant attention.

Change the subject, she told herself. She cast her glance around the room, looking behind her, focusing on anything and everything that wasn't Ash.

When she saw the side table by the door, she had it.

"Hey. Did you..."

Hmm.

Changing the subject was a good idea.

Flat out accusing one of the fae of taking something from her apartment might not be.

Too bad that Ash wasn't about to let it go. "Did I what?"

Oh, well. In for a penny, in for a pound.

She shrugged, only to aware of the way his eyes followed the motion of her tits bobbing up and down. "Mitch is missing his watch. I was just wondering if you know what happened to it."

Ash blinked. For the first time, he looked her in the face. "Are you accusing me of stealing from a human?"

"Not accusing you, no. But you were here, so was Mitch's watch, then you were both gone. I just thought I'd ask and— *oh*."

He was so very quick. Ash's moves were deceptively graceful, turning him into an even more elite predator. In the blink of an eye, he crossed the distance between them, coming within inches of her. He didn't touch her, not quite, but they were so close that if she just breathed wrong, her boobs would graze the front of his white uniform-like shirt with the array of golden buttons keeping it fastened.

She noticed the shiny buttons mainly because, as soon as she blinked and saw him *right there*, she squeaked and dropped her gaze as if unprepared to see the lust in the depths of his matching eyes. Then *her* eyes dropped further and, all of a sudden, she paid attention to the sword hanging in a white leather sheath at his hip.

That did it. Callie backed up hurriedly.

Unlike the fae, she wasn't graceful in the least. After a few frantic steps, she lost her footing in a bid to put more of the hall between them. The apartment tilted sideways and, the next thing she knew, she was flat on her ass.

And Ash was right in front of her again.

She would've thought that the roaring heat would dim to simmer after the way she wiped out like that. And maybe it would have if Callie hadn't landed with her legs spread open, giving Ash a direct peek at the teensy, tiny scrap of underwear that barely covered her pussy.

She closed her legs.

Ash gave her a long-suffering sigh, then moved toward her before holding out his hand. "Allow me to help you up."

His fingers were long, almost unnaturally so. It had the same richly bronzed skin as the rest of him, including his palm. It was one point on Ash that was so very *other* that she remembered just in time that he was fae.

And hadn't she heard long ago to never give the fae permission to touch you?

It was a buried memory that had made itself

known yesterday. Something kept telling her to keep her distance, and during her reading of a few of the fairy books she kept on her bookshelf, there were passing mentions made of that very same warning.

Callie shook her head. "I'm good."

"Give me your hand, Callie."

That sounded like a command to her. Good thing that Callie wasn't her true name, huh.

Pushing herself to her feet, she refused again. "I'm fine. You don't have to pretend to be a gentleman."

"Is that so?" Ash frowned. "Haven't you forgotten? I can't pretend at all when you're near."

"That's just your glamour," she brushed off, feeling suddenly annoyed. So they were back to 'human' again now? She supposed she deserved it, but still. "I can see through that, but that's all I can really do. How can I trust you? You could be lying right to my face and I'd never know."

Ash's expression turned to one of scrutiny again.

Callie didn't like it. "What?"

"It's just that you called me fae. I thought you knew all about my people."

"Okay. Now what does *that* mean?"

He turned away from her.

Callie clenched her teeth. If there was one thing that drove her nuts, it was when someone turned their back on her when she was talking to them. Growing up the youngest of three, Ariadne and Hope used to do it to her all the damn time. It was infuriating. And maybe she'd started it by throwing down the gauntlet when it came to not being able to trust him, but he was fae! How was she supposed to trust a fae she just met, even if he did save her?

"I asked you a question, Ash. I know you're fae. I know you're from Faerie. Excuse me if I don't know much more than that, but when most of the faerie creatures I run into are, I don't know, actively trying to *hunt* me, forgive me for not asking them all about their differences. I'm human, as you keep reminding me. I shouldn't know about Faerie. You're lucky I know as much as I do."

That caught his attention. Slowly turning on his heel, Ash's expression this time was unreadable.

He bowed his head slightly. "So I am. If you don't know that the fae are incapable of telling a lie, then it would follow that you'd doubt my word. And perhaps you should. While every word I speak is true, things aren't always as they seem. But believe me when I tell you this: there's a reason we've met. I don't know what that is just yet, but I will figure it out. Until then, I'm not going anywhere. You might as well get used to it."

Callie was silent for a moment. It was good to hear that the fae were forced to tell *a* truth if not *the* truth, but for Ash to smugly tell her that she had no choice in the matter now that he had fixated on her?

"What the— *no*. It doesn't work like that. This is my

apartment. My *home*. I let you in today"—because, to the twisty fae, her opening the door probably counted, even if he swept in without an actual invitation—"but that doesn't mean I'll always be available to humor you. I have a life. A job. I don't have time to deal with an arrogant fae male I just met."

"You make excellent points there. To them, I have one thing to say. Leave all of your human responsibilities behind. Come with me to Faerie. Maybe things will be much clearer there."

Callie blinked. Oh. Look at that. Now they were back to this beautiful male being certifiable again, weren't they?

"No."

He pursed his lips, an expression that somehow made him seem even more stunning. Probably because it just highlighted the cutting edge of his cheekbones, she decided.

"You do so love to refuse me."

She shrugged. "That's the great thing about being human. I get a choice. It's this amazing thing called free will. You should try it some time."

It was, on the surface, a flippant comment, but Callie was testing him. She needed to know just how much trouble she was in now that he'd come to see her again.

"I get what I want eventually, *human*. You'd do well to remember that."

She raised her eyebrows. A tricky fae answer. She should've expected as much.

Well, two could play that game.

"And you'd do well to remember that my name isn't 'human'. I don't know what it is you want from me, but—"

"That again? You still don't know what I want?" Ash scoffed. Damn it, even *that* was attractive. "You seem a grown human to me. Untouched, yes, but I didn't take you for an innocent. You must know."

Callie fisted her hands at her hips.

"I'm no innocent," she retorted. "And I don't know where you get off calling me 'untouched' like that since my sex life sure as hell isn't any of your business—"

His golden eyes lit up with a predatory gleam. "Oh, but it is now."

Callie pointedly ignored that. "—but, anyway, I'm no virgin, either. You're right. I don't know that much about your people. I told you before, you're the first fae that's actually spoken to me. But I'm a pretty girl basically on her own in a big city. I've dealt with my fair share of pervs. If you think you can waltz in her and expect that I'm going to fuck you, then I'm sorry. You're wasting your time."

"Am I?" Ash sidled closer. "You owe me a debt."

She'd been wondering when he would bring that up. It wasn't an accident that he didn't mention it before now. She was sure of that.

"So you want to have sex, is that it? You saved my life, so now I have to sleep with you or... what? You'll kill me?"

Because, to Callie, the literal meaning of a life debt was just that. He saved her life and now her life was forfeit to him. If Ash pushed it, he could twist it so that her murder would be justified—well, to a fae, it would be.

"I won't take your body or your life, but I'll settle on a piece of your soul. Give me that, and the debt's even. Then we can discuss fucking each other—because, I promise you, Callie, that we will eventually... once we're on a more equal footing, of course. We owe each other nothing except honesty. I can't lie to you and I expect you to treat me the same." He paused for a moment, letting his words break through the sudden shock clouding her mind. "Do we have an agreement?"

Putting aside his absolute certainty that they would end up in bed together, Callie just resisted the urge to gape up at him. Ever since the event in the park, she had decided he had only followed her home to make sure he could collect on his life debt. Sure, she began to see—even without relying on her sight—that there was more to it than that now that he'd come back again, but to just put his intentions out there like that?

And if he really couldn't lie to her, then he meant every last word he said—including that he would wipe the life debt clear for a piece of her soul.

If only she knew that *that* meant.

"I'm not agreeing to anything just yet," she said carefully, "but say I did. What does it mean, give you a piece of my soul?"

"It's very, very simple. You give me permission to touch you. Nothing intimate," he added before she could interject again, "though it certainly can be. A brush of your hand against mine will do, my fingers against your cheek... there has to be a touch. I won't take much. You'll hardly miss it. But for one of my kind, it'll give me a rush of power and a pleasure that's almost as good as sex. You'll experience the pleasure, too, so don't fret that it'll hurt."

"And... and that's all? You touch me and then I won't have to worry about the life debt anymore?"

"I told you that I couldn't lie, didn't I?"

True.

And Callie really, really hoped she could believe that.

7

Callie couldn't see that she had any other choice.

Free will? What free will? It might appear like she actually had a say in the matter, but Ash had maneuvered her so expertly that she felt like her back was up against the wall.

"Fine. If it'll mean that I won't have you holding your saving my life over my head, then fine. You can touch me."

"I have your permission?"

She nodded, but before Ash could move into her, she held up her hand. "Hang on. What would happen if you touched me and you didn't have it?"

Ash hesitated for a moment, before admitting, "I would burn. I'd get no power out of it, no strength, and

I would burn where I touched you. The human soul means nothing to my kind if it isn't freely given."

"So you can't just grab me. I have to give you the okay?"

"That's right. But if you touch me and think that it'll hurt me, know that any touch you give has your permission. It's only stolen touches that cause me pain. And, believe me, I abhor pain of any kind."

Good to know. "I give you permission for one touch then," she said, offering him the top of her hand. "To complete my debt."

She should've known better. Barely a day after they actually met, she should've figured that Ash wasn't the type to run his fingers across her hand and leave it at that. He'd spent their short acquaintance already pushing her as far as he could. Why wouldn't he do that now?

Instead of taking her hand, Ash leaned over Callie, pressing the palm of his hand to the back of her neck. Slowly, he applied enough pressure to tilt her head back so that she was forced to watch his gaze heat up, his lips curling in an almost feral smile as he reached deep inside of her and plucked out the piece of soul she so readily offered up to him.

It was a good thing he was supporting her neck. As the rush of pleasure washed over her, her knees went weak. As he touched her, Ash was the only thing keeping her from falling back to the ground.

Almost as good as sex? Ash was selling himself short since, one quick touch, and Callie was on the edge of being orgasmic.

"Whoa," she breathed out as she locked eyes with him.

That's all she could mutter.

Whoa.

And then it was done.

Ash took his hand away from her skin with the utmost reluctance. He wasn't kidding when he said he got a jolt of power from just brushing his hand against her. His skin, already so sun-drenched, seemed to glow; his golden eyes did, too. Everything about him was thrown in sharp relief and, unless she was imagining it, he was just about vibrating in place.

He cleared his throat. And that's when he said, almost solemnly: "The debt is paid. You no longer owe me for saving you life."

"Um. Okay." She hesitated a moment, then asked, "Um. Where are you going?"

Because he was already halfway toward the front door.

"I must return to Faerie. I must return to my post. It's for the best."

She felt dazed. Confused. Part of her wondered if she'd been duped, and an even more insistent part wanted to beg Ash to stay.

If he touched her again, she'd fuck him. As simple

as that. She felt so aroused, so hot, so *achy* that another touch would make her lose control—and that's assuming she had any to begin with.

He had to go. He was right. It *was* for the best. But as he backed toward the door, Callie couldn't help but ask, "Will I ever see you again?"

She should've been made leery of the way his eyes went impossibly bright. The tips of his pointed ears peeked through his long, tawny hair and, holy shit, they were *twitching* in open excitement. Her gaze darting low, drawn to the undeniable bulge pushing against his tight uniform pants, she was stunned to see that his ears weren't the only part of him affected by their touch.

"Oh, Callie," he purred in a husky voice, "now that I've marked you, you couldn't *keep* me away."

AND THEN, quickly conjuring that same faerie fire, he drew a large rectangular shape in front of him. Instead of shoving something inside of it like he had the burlap sack with the kobold's body in it, he snapped his finger and the whole damn thing erupted into a wall of red and white and orange flames.

Callie gasped. "What the—"

"Until we meet again," Ash said before he walked straight into the fire.

A moment later, the fire winked out. Just like yesterday, he was gone.

And Callie was sure she'd finally figured out what he meant by Light Fae portal.

ASH'S PORTAL brought him to another part of the Iron. Using glamour to keep from frightening any worthless human that might be around, he landed softly on the grass and blinked, still partly stunned from his realization.

Callie was his *ffrindau*.

It wasn't supposed to be possible. A human destined to be the fated mate to a Light Fae? In his three centuries, he'd heard whispers of it happening, but while many fae entertained themselves with a little human bedsport, he'd never met a fae who'd bonded with a human before *because it wasn't supposed to be possible*.

Of course, he had suspected it. If anyone would've asked him, he would've bluffed and twisted his words so that they took it as a denial. But he *had* suspected it before purposely shoving the suspicion far from him.

There was a thin line between love and hate, even thinner than the veil that often separated two totally different realms. In his case, while the fae couldn't tell a lie, it appeared it was entirely possible to lie to themselves since Ash had been convinced that he hated his white-haired human.

And then his instincts kicked in right as the kobold tore off toward her, and he realized that the fact that he regarded Callie as 'his' even then should've been a clue that things weren't as they seemed.

Now there was no denying it. He could have excused the way his body reacted, his cock going instantly hard when he found Callie half-dressed. She was an attractive human and, fae or not, he was a healthy male. He'd have to be dead not to be aroused. But then he sacrificed the life debt for a touch and, well, that was that.

If he'd been ignoring what was in front of his face, he didn't have the luxury of that any longer. One touch and everything was different. Everything changed.

He had a mate, and she was a human who seemed to get a kick out of refusing him.

Rejecting him.

Ash might be more concerned about that if there weren't a few things about being touched by a fae that he had neglected to mention. Oh, the simple transfer of her bright soul into a being designed to be soulless was as powerful as he boasted, but there was more to it than that. It was a tether between the two of them that would only be second to their fated mate bond, and now that she'd let him in, Ash could find her wherever she went. Plus, there was the addictive quality to a fae's touch. Callie would start to crave it which meant that she'd be a lot more open to his being around.

Since she'd quickly shut down his offer to take her to Faerie, he knew he would have to spend as much time as he could in her iron cage of an apartment. He hoped that, sooner or later, he could convince her to join him in his world; after all, once he had claimed her fully, she'd have to follow him home. Born with the sight as she was, Callie belonged to Faerie. It wouldn't be as dangerous for her as it would an ordinary human, and now that Ash had imprinted on her, she'd never have anything to fear.

He would always protect his human, whether she wanted him to or not.

For now, though, she belonged in the Iron. He wouldn't bother asking her again to join him in Faerie since it was clear what her answer would be. Kidnapping her and spiriting her away would only put a wrench in his new plan to claim her as his mate.

And despite not having the gift of her true name, now that it was undeniable that she was his *ffrindau*, he couldn't compel her to do anything that she didn't want to.

The touch might've given him some power over her, but her sight had always awarded her some protection. The truth of who she was to him awarded her even more. As much as it pained him to admit, a

Light Fae was on the same level as one of the mortal humans.

Then again, that was how it should be between mates. If not equal, then she should be put on a pedestal, better than he deserved and too, too good for the likes of him.

He'd take her anyway, though. He'd take her any way he could until she consented and gave him the final touch that would make her irrevocably his.

Well, at least he finally understood why he'd been so drawn to her from the first moment their eyes met. That simple touch confirmed something that the rest of him had guessed long before now.

Callie was meant for him, which—to Ash—meant that no one else should have her.

It was still daylight. He had hours of human time left before he'd have to return to Faerie, and while he was buzzing, his cock still hard, his very instincts urging him to go back to Callie, it wasn't the hairbrush he pulled out of his pocket. Before he touched Callie, he could've used her brush and her pretty strands of pale hair to chase her across her human world; now he could use the tether of their shared touch. He'd keep it anyway, a token of his female, but he kept it in his pocket with Nine's pebble.

Instead, he grabbed the cheap, broken timepiece with its falsely leather band.

Mitch.

The male whose essence and aura mingled throughout the apartment with Callie's. Every time Ash's heightened senses picked up on it, he'd barely been able to refrain from baring his teeth at the hint of a male daring to encroach on his female. Human or not, he was still a threat.

For a fae soldier, there was only one way to eliminate a threat.

But Callie was human. This Mitch was obviously human, too. In the Iron, he knew the humans tended to massacre each other even more mercilessly than in Faerie, but he carried a piece of Callie's soul inside of him now. Her response at his touch told Ash that he would be able to seduce his mate eventually, but if he killed that male?

She'd never let him touch her again.

Good thing that Ash was clever. Tricky. Determined.

And he had a watch that would lead him to the human, and whatever glamour it took to convince this Mitch to leave Callie in his care.

After all, he was her mate. No one would take better care of her than he would.

ASH TOLD her that the fae couldn't lie, and he also told her that she wouldn't be able to keep him away.

Three days after he left her apartment, Callie was beginning to think one of the two things couldn't be true since there had been no sign of Ash since.

She couldn't understand why she wanted him to visit her again so badly. Though she didn't expect him to show up at Buster's or anything, he wasn't at the park when she purposely stopped by, and if her heart-beat picked up whenever someone approached her apartment, disappointment set in every time that it wasn't her golden fae.

She should've known better. If that touch felt as good to him as it did to her, he'd probably gotten what he wanted out of her already. Then again, he *had* made it clear that he wouldn't settle for less than getting into her bed, so maybe she was just being an idiot for hoping that he'd come and see her again.

But he hadn't, and on the fourth evening, she huffed and drowned her sorrows in a pint of ice cream.

Add that to how strange Mitch had been acting lately, and Callie was feeling more than a little alone. She blamed it on the pressures at his office since her roommate seemed to be almost living downtown. Over four days, she'd seen him for maybe a grand total of twenty minutes. He looked pale and wan, a glazed look in his deep brown eyes, and dark purple circles under-lining them. She didn't want to bother him, so she made quick small talk and just reminded Mitch that she was there for him.

Maybe when he finally got that promotion, she could take him out to celebrate. Kill two birds with one stone and all that. Show Mitch she was happy for him while also getting out instead of waiting around for Ash to reappear.

The next morning was her off day and though it was out of the ordinary for Callie, she allowed herself to really sleep in. It was almost nine when she got up and, feeling a hunger deep in her gut, decided to make breakfast.

Ha. As if food would feed the craving she hadn't been able to kick yet.

She wanted dick. Plain and simple. And though she knew Mitch would shuck his boxers and give her exactly what her body needed, the idea of banging on her roommate's door left her feeling shaky.

Damn it, she didn't want just any dick. She wanted Ash, and she blamed him for putting the idea in her head and then bailing. Not that she wanted to prove him right. He'd seemed so sure that she would come around in the end, and if she jumped him the next time he showed his gorgeous face, she could only imagine the smirk he'd pull.

Ugh.

"Get control of yourself, girl," she murmured, grabbing her hair and throwing it up in a bun.

She put on her slippers, rolling her eyes when she saw the bottoms of the sleep shorts she'd taken to wearing peeking out from under the hem of shirt. Damn it, it had barely been a week since Ash came bursting into her life and already he'd made her as nuts as she thought he was.

Whatever. If he didn't want to see her again, she couldn't make him. She'd been happy before the day she saw him standing beside that tree, and she'd be ecstatic if she never saw him again.

And if she told herself *that* enough times, maybe she'd actually believe that whopper this time around.

Since Mitch had mentioned that he wasn't going into the office today—for the first time in Callie didn't know how long—she figured he was still sleeping when she saw that his door was closed. Feeling queasy at just the thought of knocking on it even though she'd never turn to her friend just to scratch this crazy itch, she shuffled past it.

Still, she was heading to make breakfast. She might as well see if he wanted any.

"Mitch?" she called out. "I'm gonna make some waffles. You want some?"

No answer.

He must still be sleeping, she mused. Good. He needed the rest.

She milled around the kitchen, pulling out all of the ingredients she would need to make waffles. For some strange reason, it looked like there were fewer things in the pantry, the drawers, the fridge than there had been before. Maybe it was time to take a run to the grocery store. Might as well since she didn't really have anything else to do today, and going to the park to take more photographs just didn't appeal to her at the moment.

As she went to the cabinet where she swore she kept their waffle iron, she noticed that it wasn't just food that was missing. The whole kitchen looked different. Something... something wasn't right. It took her longer than it should've to notice that Mitch's cast iron pan was missing, especially since it had been so handy the other day against Ash.

Not that she was planning on threatening him with it again.

If he ever showed up again, that was.

Shaking her head, she started to look for the cast iron pan. She still wasn't so sure that Ash *hadn't* snagged Mitch's watch, and though she couldn't figure out how he'd take the cast iron pan when he was clearly wary of it, maybe that was exactly why it was gone now.

Sure, she might—against her better judgment—want to fuck Ash, but she'd be a moron to trust anything he said.

After another search, she realized that there was no sign of the cast iron pan. Even weirder, that wasn't the only other item that was gone. Mitch's knife set. His favorite cereal bowl. The set of good glasses that he kept for when Tony and Ariadne came by for dinner.

Ignoring the sinking suspicion in the pit of her stomach, she left the kitchen, heading for the bathroom they shared.

Everything that Mitch used was gone.

What the—

Though it took every ounce of will Callie had, she went to his bedroom. The suspicion had ramped up to a burst of anxiety she couldn't ignore so, instead of knocking, she threw open the door.

There was a mattress in there.

That was all.

A *mattress.*

No bedding. No blankets. No pillows.

Callie darted in, yanking open his closet door. Not even a hanger lingered inside.

"Mitch?"

She had a phone in her room. Trading Mitch's for hers, Callie grabbed the handset and dialed his cellphone number, grateful she had memorized it.

Of course the fucker was off. Why wouldn't it be when it seemed as if her closest friend had up and disappeared without a word?

Slamming down the phone, she tried in vain to make sense of what had happened. Because it didn't make *any* sense at all. It was like Mitch had taken everything he owned with him overnight, moving out without saying a damn thing, and he would never, ever do that... would he?

She thought about calling her sister, maybe having Ariadne ask Tony about Mitch. Since that would inevitably lead to everyone losing their shit if they didn't know, she decided to wait until she could get in touch with him first. The phone wasn't on right now, but it would be eventually, right?

And then she'd make him explain.

Because this? It was inexplicable.

Callie stormed out of her room. She wasn't sure if she was surprised or angry or just confused. Mostly confused, she decided, and definitely not hungry any longer. She headed back toward the kitchen, determined to put away all of the ingredients she had taken out—and that's when she noticed the envelope with her name scrawled in Mitch's sloppy handwriting on it.

It was resting on the back of the couch. He probably thought she couldn't miss it, but she obviously had.

Until now.

Her heart racing, pulse pounding, Callie snatched the envelope and tore it open. If he thought he could explain the way he dipped out so suddenly in a letter, then he had another think coming.

And then she read the single page he'd tucked inside, and it suddenly made just a little more sense.

8

The first time Callie saw Ash conjure a portal, she'd been amazed after she got over her surprise.

The second?

She barely paid it any attention.

Still stunned by Mitch's note, she felt the air shift in the hallway a few seconds before the rush of warmth licked at her back.

Ash murmured a soft greeting.

He didn't knock, she noticed. Five days since she last saw him and he came with barely a 'hello' and no pretenses whatsoever that she could actually keep the powerful fae out even if she wanted to. It had been barely a week since the first time she spotted him lurking on the edge of the park and already Ash had made himself at home in her apartment.

Her apartment. Not *their* apartment. And all because Mitch had suddenly decided that he needed to head back to the suburbs.

Coincidence? If only she was the type of girl who believed in coincidences. It seemed too much to be one, but Mitch made it clear in his letter. He promised to keep paying his half of the rent until she could find a new roommate, but he'd learned earlier this week that he was denied the promotion. Worse, his start-up company expected him to keep up the same level of work with a notable pay cut.

The stress had broken her poor friend. Too embarrassed and ashamed to tell her the truth, he'd spent the last few days making arrangements to move in with his parents. She shouldn't blame her sister for not telling her sooner since he'd made his mom and dad swear not to let his brother or his wife know. It was bad enough he'd felt like he had to abandon Callie and the city. The last thing he wanted was to deal with Tony telling him "I told you so".

He didn't answer his cellphone because he didn't have it anymore. He turned it in when he quit his job. And until he could get his head screwed on straight, he was begging Callie not to call him at his parents' home. He'd get in touch with her when he felt like he could face her again but, until then, the money would be in their rent account for the first every month.

He swore it.

Too bad that Callie didn't give a shit about the money. She just wanted her friend to be okay. And if that meant giving him his space, she would—and when she heard from him again, she'd rip him a goddamn new one for feeling like he had to sneak out in the middle of the night like some kind of thief or something.

So maybe Callie couldn't help but wonder if Mitch had a push out the door. On two separate occasions Ash had made it clear that he wanted Mitch gone... but he wouldn't really have done something about it, would he?

No. No, Callie told herself. How could he? Mitch had been working toward this promotion for months, long before that June day when she first spotted Ash in the park. Mitch had known it was only a chance even then, and he'd always been a bit overdramatic. She could totally buy him turning tail and running home again when they denied him.

She sighed and, shoving the letter she'd read countless times that morning back into its envelope, turned to look behind her at Ash.

The reality of Mitch leaving had one bonus. Since this morning, she'd managed to wrangle her lusty libido under control. She'd showered, dressed, and plopped herself on the couch without sex—or Ash—crossing her mind again. Looking at him now, she appreciated how gorgeous, if aloof, he was, but she could smile at him without wondering what he looked like under the same white trimmed with gold uniform he always wore.

"Something wrong, Callie?"

At least he wasn't starting up with that 'human' BS again. They were beyond that now. She could see the truth of that written on his flawless features. The touch they shared had done something to them both, and she probably would've been more worried about that realization if it wasn't for Mitch's sudden disappearance.

She set the envelope down on the couch cushion. "Hey. You wouldn't happen to be looking for a place in the human world, would you?"

"Excuse me?"

"Nothing. Forget about it."

"But I don't want to," he told her, a sly smile tugging on his lips. Her stomach flip-flopped. "Are you inviting me to stay?"

"What? No. It's just... I'm out one roommate." She watched him closely, looking for a reaction she instinctively knew she'd never get. He didn't disappoint, either. "It's fine. I'll be fine. It was just a joke."

"If you mean you finally got rid of that male like I told you to, then I'm glad. But let's get back to your request. Are you asking me if I'd stay the night with you?"

His lyrical voice was almost a purr.

Callie thought of the way she went all hot and liquid-y at his touch. In an instant, Mitch was shoved to the back of her mind—and that probably should've worried her a bit, too.

"That's not what I—"

"I'm a creature of Faerie, a member of the Summer Court. A Light Fae, Callie. A Blessed One. I can only cross into the Iron during the daylight," Ash explained. "When the shadows fall, I must return. I could never stay the night with you."

"I didn't—"

"But," he continued, as if she hadn't said a word, "we don't need the night. Now that the other male is gone, we can share our days together. Come with me."

"Wait." She blinked. Maybe she was still pretty horny, and she was definitely not in the best state of mind right now, but she'd been half-expecting him to proposition her. Especially the way he said *come* like that, only that wasn't the vibe she got from him. Was she wrong? "What?"

"Come with me."

"What type of 'coming' are we talking about?"

Ash laughed. It struck her then that that was the first time she ever heard his laugh. It was clear, almost crystal-like, and it delighted her in a way she would've thought impossible the first time she read Mitch's goodbye letter.

"I'm willing to wait for what you have in your mind,

dear Callie. You weren't lying when you told me you were no innocent, but that can wait. Let me seduce you. Let me make you want my touch. Let me get to know you, and show you that I'm more than what you think I am. I beg of you, don't refuse me again. You won't regret saying 'yes.'"

Callie wasn't so sure of that. And, yet, her knee-jerk reaction to reject this fae male was nowhere near as strong as it had been.

"Okay. Say I bite. You want me to come with you. I assume you mean a place. So where? Where are we going?" she asked, not even trying to hide her suspicion. He hadn't tried to convince her to visit Faerie with him again, but that didn't mean she believed he gave up on the idea.

Which was why she was surprised when his eyes brightened.

"Wherever you want to go, my *ffrindau*."

She didn't have half a clue what that meant, but it sounded so much like 'friend' that it had to be that.

Friend.

She could use a friend right now.

"You know what? Okay. Let's go."

———

"IT'S ALMOST SUNDOWN."

Ash joined Callie at her living room window. "So it is."

It was the end of July. She'd lost track of how many times they'd ended another afternoon together at this very same window, watching the sun threaten to separate them. Only it wasn't a threat so much as it was a promise since Ash would have to leave before the sun completely set and night fell.

Since he'd come to see her more regularly, her fae had explained how the iron in the human world affected him, how his magic and his aura interfered with her tech—specifically her lightbulbs and her appliances—and how the shadows on her side of the veil were more poisonous than those in Faerie. If he stayed, he'd weaken so greatly that there was a chance he'd never be able to create another portal to return to his world again.

So he had to return. He also finally admitted what he was doing in that hazy patch the day they met. He was a fae soldier, serving the most powerful fae in all of Faerie —Melisandre, the Fae Queen—and while he wasn't in battle or guarding his queen, he was posted along the borders, protecting Faerie from any intruders that might make their way through the thinnest points of the veil. Just like she guessed, the patch marked a breach between worlds, and he'd been guarding it when he first caught sight of Callie and knew that she was different.

To Ash, she couldn't help being human anymore than he could help obeying the rise and fall of the sun. He'd never use the word *weakness*, but she knew how he felt and decided early on that she had to accept him for what he was unless she wanted to say goodbye.

Not that she expected he'd *let* her, but since he never forced her to do anything she didn't want to, she knew her rejection would hurt him more than it would amuse him now that she'd learned to know more about him.

Lately, though, Ash had been staying longer and longer, pushing his return to Faerie back. He confessed he felt unsettled when they apart, and wished they didn't have to be. Surprisingly, he didn't bring up her visiting Faerie again, and when she subtly mentioned that it wouldn't be that big of a deal being locked out of Faerie if he decided to stay with *her*, Ash didn't deny it.

In fact, he said, "Perhaps. At any rate, maybe I should learn about the world that has your heart. You belong in the Iron. I'd like to understand why."

So she brought him to movie matinees, trying not to laugh when the projector gave out halfway after Ash's aura surged during one of the horror scenes. They went out to lunch, sharing human food while Ash told Callie solemnly never to accept or eat food from Faerie unless she never wanted to experience the deliciousness that was pepperoni pizza ever again.

They went for afternoon strolls around the city,

helping Ash build his tolerance to the iron that surrounded them. It was at his insistence, too, since he didn't want it to ever come between the two of them.

Most of all, though, they spent a lot of their time in her apartment together talking. Mainly because Ash did better when they were alone without an audience of humans gawking at him in the glamour he adopted to fit in, but also because he liked having all of her attention on him.

Especially after an incident that took place at the movie theatre. Right before previews started, Callie went to run to the bathroom and then get some popcorn for Ash to try. From experience, she knew he'd come looking for her if she took too long—no matter where she was or where she went, he had a knack for tracking her down—and she tried to brush off the guy flirting with her while she was waiting for her corn to finish popping.

When he didn't get the hint, she tried to move away from him. The guy didn't like that and he lashed out, grabbing Callie's arm to keep her from walking away from him.

Before she could break his hold, Ash appeared like an avenging angel. He grabbed the man's hand and squeezed. There was a cracking sound, almost like bones breaking, but Ash met the guy's suddenly dilated eyes and said, voice layered with both glamour and suggestion, "Scream and I'll rip your testicles off."

Poor guy didn't even whimper.

Ash squeezed his hand again. More cracking. More breaking.

He shoved the man away from Callie. "Now go."

He did. Moving as if the hounds of hell were after him, the jerk tore out of the cineplex. No one stopped him, just like no one regarded Ash with anything other than shock and awe—which he took as his due, of course.

Ash held out his hand. Callie winced when she saw the shiny pink skin, burned raw but healing quickly. Blisters formed then faded as she watched.

Her fae smiled over at her. "Come. The movie's getting ready to begin. I didn't want you to miss it."

Without even thinking about her popcorn, she slipped her hand in Ash's waiting palm and headed toward the theatre.

AFTER A FEW WEEKS, and many more lonely nights, she had to admit they were dating. Ash still referred to it as studying the Iron, trying to understand her fascination with the human world, but Callie knew what it was even if her haughty Light Fae male didn't: they were dating, and she wasn't sure how much longer it was going to last.

He seemed so into her, but Callie had had guys that

were super devoted until they got what they wanted and then, as if overnight, they weren't.

Still, he was definitely jealous. Once she broke through his icy facade, Callie realized that he blazed as hot as the sun that gave him his power. Even though she'd finally talked to Mitch and he assured her that he was home and he was happy—though he regretted the cowardly way he left—she still couldn't help but think, "I wonder."

I wonder if Ash had something to do with it.

I wonder if I'm falling too hard too fast.

I wonder if I'm fooling myself.

If she wasn't, she was definitely fooling nearly everyone else around her. Buster, who met her new "friend" after her fae spent hours guarding the bench outside of Buster's Photo while she worked. Her parents who could never get her on the phone, and when they did, quizzed her on who she was spending time with and what she was doing since Mitch wasn't there anymore. Hope, who offered to keep her company while she looked for a roommate, and who threw a snit when Callie refused to let her.

She was used to lying. It came from a lifetime of denying the things she saw if only to put her parents and her sisters' minds at ease.

But when it came to Ash, she always told the truth. She felt it was only fair. As one of the fae, he couldn't lie to her. Oh, he could be tricky—and he often was—

but he was often honest to a fault. The least she could do was be truthful in return.

Which was why when, about a month and a half after their fateful meeting, she nearly lost her mind when she realized that while Ash was forced by magic to always tell the truth, it didn't mean that he was as honest as she thought he was.

His seduction was working. Between the small, intimate touches they shared—always with her permission—and the way he did everything to prove that he was a good match for her despite being fae, she'd had her cravings for him sated enough that they didn't need to take the next step just yet.

They both recognized that the prospect of sex had gone from a possibility to an eventuality, but there was no reason to rush. As an immortal fae with no real concept of time, he was content to wait until Callie was ready. And now that she saw him much more frequently, she could tolerate the gaps when time ran differently and he was in Faerie for longer than they both wanted him to be.

It was those gaps that were bothering Ash. She thought his protective nature had something to do with his being a soldier, but though he insisted he couldn't stay in the Iron for more than a few hours at a time, he was worried about Callie when he *wasn't* with her.

While the fae were limited to the times they could

cross into the Iron, most found it too bothersome. They preferred to stay in Faerie, and while a few went hunting for a human companion willing to touch them, it was the lower races of Faerie who would risk the Iron rather than live under Melisandre's cruel reign.

Callie thought she understood. "Like that kobold, right?"

Ash couldn't lie, but as she got to know him, she got to understand that he had tells. A way for her to know when he was saying one thing but meaning another, the faerie equivalent to fibbing.

Which was exactly what he did when he said, "The kobold was a threat, yes."

A casual comment. Only... Callie felt her bullshit meter going off.

But why?

Unless—

The burlap sack. The one Ash had used to get rid of the kobold's remains. Why did she only just now remember that, seconds before the kobold broke through the veil, she saw Ash holding that same sack?

Oh, no.

It couldn't be—

Could it?

9

S wallowing roughly, trying to stay calm, Callie said, "I wonder how it managed to escape the veil in the first place. I mean, that's what you were there for. Guarding the weak point in the veil. Keeping humans out." She met his gaze. "Keeping dangerous faerie creatures in."

Ash didn't say anything.

No, but his silence did.

"Ash... you didn't."

"Didn't do what?"

No. He didn't get to pretend. He didn't get to conveniently misunderstand, or twist it around so that she was imagining things.

Concrete answer. She needed a concrete answer.

"Yes or no. Tell me right now. You had something to

do with that. With the kobold getting out and coming after me."

"Callie—"

"Don't you 'Callie' me, Ash. Yes or no."

He didn't break the stare, even as he nodded. "Yes."

She gritted her teeth. "Explain."

And, for better or for worse, he did.

Furious was too soft a word for what she was as he finished talking. He didn't ask for forgiveness or even try to make it seem like anything other than a callous decision he'd made once upon a time. To Ash, it was the perfect choice.

To Ash.

Not to Callie.

She got up from the couch, shoving away from it just in time to miss the brush of his fingers as he reached for her.

"Don't touch me," she snapped.

Ash fisted his fingers. "I killed it for you. That should count for something."

Oh? Should it?

"You killed it, then made me give you my name in order to get rid of its body. Listen to me. *It*. Like that makes it any better that you killed a living being as... as a test."

"That's not what happened."

"It's not? You just told me that you were either hoping I'd pass or that poor thing would kill me. You set us both up. Because I thought you saved my life by ending the kobold's. That's how you tricked me into letting you touch me the first time—"

"It wasn't a trick," Ash argued. "You accepted the deal."

At that moment, Callie fervently wished that Mitch hadn't taken his cast iron pan with him when he left. Right then? She was so fucking pissed, she thought she might actually bean Ash dead in his perfect face with it.

Instead, she pointed at the door. "Get out."

"Callie—"

"I can't force you. Maybe I've been pretending all along that I had some power in this relationship, but if you stay here, you'll just show me that I never should've let you follow me home in the first place. Take a portal. Use the door. I don't give a shit. Just... just go."

She was so very angry, but some other emotion bubbled up and out of her chest as she jabbed her pointer finger at the door again. As she told him to leave, her voice broke.

It was that more than anything else that had Ash rising from the couch and, within seconds, disappearing through another of his Light Fae portals.

Ash didn't stay gone for long.

Honestly, she hadn't expected him to. As angry as she was, it was both her day off and barely morning when the two of them had sat down on the couch and started to talk. Arrogant as ever, she didn't really think he would honor her request if only because there were hours until he was forced to return, and he wouldn't want to miss out on any time he had with her.

As much as didn't want to admit it, the Ash she knew lately was different from the haughty prick who followed her home after he slayed the kobold. That's what made her so mad, though. Because she didn't want to believe that the male she had fallen for was still the heartless fae who thought he could solve his curiosity with a little mayhem and murder.

Callie knew what she was getting into when she started dating a fae. At least, she *thought* she had.

Considering she was marching around the kitchen, slamming cabinets, banging things, and pointedly ignoring the way she could just... just *know* that Ash had returned to the apartment, she wasn't so sure that was the case.

She wasn't hungry, but hell if she would let him think that she was still stewing over their argument. Though he never came out and said it, she knew Ash thought of her emotional outbursts as just part of her being human. God forbid one of the fae act anything other than haughty and in control. He probably would expect her to be fuming, and she wanted him to think she could shake it off as easily as he could.

So, refusing to look behind her to where Ash was looming in the doorway, she grabbed a Lean Cuisine from the freezer, ripped it open, then tossed it into the microwave. A blank display greeted her when she went to enter the time.

Great. Just *great*.

Yanking on the handle, she snatched the microwaveable meal and shoved it back in the freezer. She closed the freezer door, then used the flat of her hand to slam the open microwave door shut.

"Be careful. You could break that."

Callie scoffed. "Too late. It's already dead."

"I'll get you another."

Of course he would. How he got his hands on human money, she had no idea, but Ash was very generous with it. He offered to pay for their outings, though Callie insisting on trading off, but when it came to replacing any of the appliances his appearance tended to short out, she had no problem accepting that kind of money from him.

This would be the third microwave. She was on her fifth coffeemaker. And lightbulbs? Phew. The poor clerk probably wondered what the hell she was doing with all of the things she kept replacing, but she hadn't cared. It had been worth it to spend time with Ash.

Or she thought.

Yup. She was still plenty pissed.

"Callie. Won't you look at me?"

She had to give him credit. Early on in their... whatever it was... Callie pointed out how much she hated him giving her orders. He did it so casually, and maybe it was one of his habits, but it drove her up the wall. He was trying to put them on an equal footing? He could start by not constantly telling her what to do.

If he had commanded her to look at him, she would've kept her back on him just for the principle of the thing. But for him to make it a request?

She turned, arms crossed over her chest.

Ash was back, and he wasn't empty-handed. A hefty bouquet of sunny yellow flowers was nestled in his arms.

"What? No roses?"

He quirked his eyebrow. "I thought you'd appreciate the freesia more." He waited a beat. "Anyone could profess their feelings with red roses. But this flower, it stands for unconditional love."

Callie almost swallowed her tongue. "Excuse me?"

Bold as brass, he added, "It works both ways, though. You knew what I was. I can't make any apologies for that. But I can promise to be better."

"Ash—"

"I have been better. I want to be the best mate I can for you. You deserve the best, and I want to make sure you have it. I might make mistakes along the way. I won't think of them like that because that's not how I'm made, but I'll listen to you when you tell me that I'm wrong. Sacrificing the kobold, putting you in danger... that was wrong. I won't do that again."

It was a start. As Callie looked at the yellow blossoms on the flowers, she accepted it was a start. To have her perfect fae admit to her that he could actually be *wrong*... hell must've frozen over because that was the last thing she ever expected to happen.

This wasn't their first fight. Hot-headed human coupled with an indifferent fae who thought he knew better... it was inevitable that they would clash. Usually, though, Callie was the one who smoothed things over because, at the end of the day, he *was* fae.

But he was a fae who could be better, and who deserved a second chance.

Unconditional love. Those flowers meant unconditional love. And *that* meant—

Callie gulped. It was too soon. Right? Too soon to talk about forever, but maybe it was right on time for something else.

Something that *she* wanted.

She lowered her hands to her hips. "Now, when you say you want to be the best mate for me, what exactly does that mean, Ash?" One look in his golden eyes and she thought she knew. "You mean... like sex? 'Mate', like the two of us doing the down and dirty, not like 'mate' as in friend, right? Fucking? You still want to fuck me?"

Ash's eyes lit up.

Oh, yeah. He definitely still wanted to do that.

Thank *God*.

She'd been waiting for him to make his move for ages now. He'd made it obvious that he was waiting for her to be ready, especially since he was the one so sure that they'd end up fucking sooner or later.

Maybe she was still a little ticked off—okay, more than a little. But the flowers had helped to dull the edge of her sharp anger, and his openness blunted it some more.

Plus, there was something about a good argument that really got her going.

During her last relationship, sometimes Callie would go so far as to pick a fight with her ex just because the make-up sex was out of this world.

And Ash? He actually *was* from another world.

In that moment, Callie made a decision that she would come to question over and over again in the not-so-distant future. But that was the future. In that moment, she was hot, she was horny, and she'd been dying to take the next step with Ash for longer than she wanted to admit.

She smiled. And if Ash looked just a little apprehensive when she turned it on him, well, *good*.

"Let me take those flowers," she said, her voice dropping lower as she sidled over to him.

He didn't resist. When she held out her hands, he placed the bouquet of flowers into her waiting arms. And if he stole the tiniest of caresses as he drew away? That just stoked the fires inside of her even higher.

"I'm going to put this in my room," she announced. Then, with a sly look over her shoulder before she left the kitchen, she added, "You're more than welcome to join me."

"Callie, there isn't anywhere I wouldn't follow you."

Her smile widened. He couldn't see it, but she was sure he noticed the swivel she put into her hips by the way he let out a soft groan.

Once inside her room, she laid the flowers on top of her dresser. She'd have to put them in water before long, but for now? She was a tad bit preoccupied.

"Ash?"

"Yes?"

"I appreciate the flowers. I really do. But, I'm wondering..."

"What are you wondering?"

"Do you really want to make this morning up to me?"

"More than anything," he vowed. "Whatever you want, you can have it. I just don't want that kobold to come between us. I don't want *anything* to come between us."

"Whatever I want, huh?" That's exactly what she was hoping he'd say. "Because what I want? Is to touch you."

For a moment, she didn't think he was going to respond. He stared at her as if he couldn't believe what his ears were telling him he had heard, but then he recovered, obviously deciding not to ask questions.

Ash opened his arms wide. "You can touch me anywhere."

"I want to touch you, but with my mouth."

Just in case he didn't get the message, she sank down easily to her knees, putting her eyes on level with the erection tenting his pants.

His expression turned hopeful, then longing.

Whoa.

Callie didn't think it was possible. Catching Ash off guard like that? Except for the first time she gave him permission to touch her, as eager as he was before he made a quick escape, he'd never acted anything less than in control around her. Letting her see his vulnerable side? She'd been convinced he didn't *have* one.

It didn't last. He recovered his arrogance almost immediately, looking down at her with a wry smile as she reached up to fist his linen pants.

His new expression told her that he definitely liked the sight of her on her knees in front of him.

If it wasn't for the fact that she was more than eager to go down on him, she might have skipped the foreplay and gone straight to the main event. But she'd had dreams about being intimate with Ash, nighttime fantasies that bled into her daydreams. She was desperate to feel his hands on her again, and while he gave her his touch, she was beginning to think that he'd never take it any farther.

Even if she just got the chance to give him pleasure, she'd take it.

Consider it her version of giving him flowers.

For a moment, he stood like... like a statue. He didn't move. He didn't blink. His golden eyes flared with something like lust, but apart from the way his Adam's apple quivered, Ash didn't react at all.

Callie tucked a lock of her white-blonde hair behind her ear. She'd given her fair share of bjs before, but it was usually the guy giving her the "go" sign that allowed her the confidence to take control of the sexual encounter.

With Ash, though, as much as she tried not to focus on it, the power imbalance was too great. Sure, her sight made it a little more even, but he was still fae. With his enhanced senses, his immortality, his glamour, compulsion, and his strength, Callie could never forget what he was—and what she wasn't.

Maybe she was being too forward. Ash had made it clear from the beginning that, whatever his reasons were, he considered Callie to belong to him. He'd been drawn to her since those early days at the park, and while she refused to ask him why, actions often spoke louder than words. He wanted her.

But did he want her like this?

Hell, what if the courtship rituals in Faerie were different? Did Ash even know what she was getting at when she said she wanted to touch him with her mouth? Maybe he thought she meant kissing, right?

What if he thought the idea of her sucking on his dick was weird?

Why was she only thinking about that now?

She swallowed roughly. There had to be a way out of this without total embarrassment. "If you don't want to—"

"I want." Ash's voice—usually so light and lyrical—came out harsh. "I very much want."

Callie raised her eyebrows. "You, um... you're sure?"

In answer, Ash curved his lips and, with a rough shove, dropped his pants down to his thighs.

His cock was already erect. Long and thicker than she would've imagined, it was a more reddish shade of his bronze-colored skin; even beneath his linen pants, he was as dark as he was everywhere else. Her mouth watered just looking at it.

"Like I told you," he grounded out. "You can touch me anywhere."

Callie wasn't fae. Unlike Ash, she didn't need to get permission to touch him. But now that she had it?

She lowered herself in front of him, steadying herself by latching onto his thighs. Even that simple touch had Ash tightening up, the rumble of pleasure starting deep in the back of his throat. His muscles went as hard as his erection. Callie stroked his skin with one hand before reaching for his cock with her other.

As Ash threw back his head, the rumble turning to a low moan, Callie smiled again. She might be the one on her knees, but there was no denying that she was the one in control. Her Light Fae handed it right over to her, and he let her keep it as she lowered her head and wrapped her lips around the head of his blazing hot cock.

From the way his body stayed tight, like a coiled spring ready to explode, Ash was working against his instincts. As she sucked and stroked and laved him with the flat of her tongue, she got the sense that he was just resisting the urge to fuck her mouth. Continuing to smile around his length, she increased the suction, inviting him to do just that.

He did. A few uncontrolled thrusts as Callie clutched his thigh tightly as she barely grazed him with her teeth.

She felt it when he let go, his splurt so powerful that she had some of his come spilling out of the corner of her mouth.

Callie swallowed as much as she could as Ash

slowly pulled his dick out from between her lips. She immediately licked the last drops away, smiling contentedly as Ash stared in amazement down at her.

Oh, yeah. That was power all right.

But Callie wasn't the only one in control. Despite his orgasm—she had the slightly salty taste in the back of her throat to prove it—Ash's dick was as hard as ever. Glistening with saliva, the thick cock bobbed gently as his chest heaved.

His voice went impossibly deeper. "Fair is fair," Ash told her. "It's my turn."

10

He reached for her, and Callie squealed as her graceful, ethereal fae nearly tripped and stumbled over the pants tangled around his calves. He shot her a heated look as he kicked them off, but still on a high from making him come so hard, she just blew him a kiss, then pulled off her t-shirt.

She tossed it on the floor. "Don't forget yours."

His pants were gone. His boots, too. But Ash was still wearing the fancy white uniform shirt with its gleaming golden buttons. It took a moment before he could rip his stare away from her cleavage and her bra and when he finally did, he glanced down at his shirt, staring at it as if he forgot how to take it off.

Callie made quick work of the rest of her clothes. She wasn't quite sure what Ash had in mind when he said it was his turn, but she was game to pretty much anything. First things first, though, she needed to be naked.

It was only as she was backing up toward the bed that it hit her what she was preparing to do.

She hesitated. Due to a bad reaction when she was a teen and she was trying to regulate her cycle, Callie wasn't on birth control. Condoms? It had been so long since she'd been with a guy, she didn't even think she had any in the apartment. Mitch always kept a box in his bedside table, but her roommate had taken everything but the furniture with him when he moved out suddenly. What were the odds he abandoned the condoms?

She was just about to excuse herself to go check when Ash finally finished unbuttoning his shirt. He let it fall, landing not too far from her discarded clothes, and her graceful Seelie was back as he swept across the room, grabbing Callie up as easily as if she were a doll before lying her gently on the bed.

With a hungry expression that had Callie's pulse kicking up, he climbed up after her, swinging a leg over her, bracing his body over hers.

She sucked in a breath, dazzled by his other-worldly beauty and the way he gobbled her up with his gaze as if he was starving and she was the only thing on the menu.

Callie opened her mouth.

Closed it.

She was human. He was fae. Their bodies were obviously compatible—even if Ash's dick was bigger than any of the other guys she'd been with before him —so sex was definitely about to happen. But they were from two different worlds. It wasn't like he could actually get her pregnant... right?

Too bad none of the books she checked out of the library covered *this* topic.

"I want to do everything with you," Ash murmured, oblivious to her inner debate. "I want to taste you. I want to touch you. I want to make you mine in every way. You're mine," he said, not for the first time. "I've waited long enough to make it undeniable. Will you open up to me, Callie? Will you let me in? Can I touch you?"

The first few times, Ash asked for permission for every touch until Callie gave him carte blanche. They were dating, after all. She never wanted him to accidentally be burned because he brushed up against her when she wasn't expecting it.

But this? This was different. Though she couldn't quite explain why, Callie knew that this was different.

"Yes, Ash," she said. "You have my permission."

That's all it took. One quick touch, making sure she was ready to receive him, and then Ash was breaching her entrance, filling her up with his length. He was even bigger inside her pussy than he'd been in her mouth, the delicious ache as he stretched her open causing Callie to let out a sound that was half-groan, half-cry of delight.

It felt so *good*.

Even better? Was when Ash started to move.

He started out slow, going easy, being gentle. Like before, though, he was coiled tight, his own instincts fighting against his ridiculous desire to treat Callie like a breakable human. He might be a nearly immortal fae with a thick cock, but he was right. She was made for him—*meant* for him.

She could take him.

"Harder," she told him. "Faster. Please, Ash. *Please...*"

"Anything for you, my mate," he said, doing just what she pleaded for. His soft thrusts became faster, deeper, his hips pistoning as his sac slammed into her ass.

Callie dug her fingers into the sheets, hanging on tightly as Ash sent her shifting along the mattress. It felt so amazing, the power of his touch reaching places inside of her that she didn't even know had been empty. Alone. Unloved. The warmth of his attention, his power, this *connection* erased all the dark, cold parts that Callie kept hidden.

As he fucked her relentlessly, she had the sudden urge to do the same for him. And, since the beginning, there was one thing Ash had demanded of her that she'd never felt secure enough to give him.

Until now.

"My name," she panted. "I want you to call me by my name."

"Callie—"

She shook her head. "No. My *full* name."

Ash stopped thrusting, his arms braced at her sides as he held himself over her. The ends of his long, tawny hair tickled her bare tits as he kept his cock buried to the hilt inside of her. But he wasn't moving.

Instead, he was staring down at Callie, an unreadable expression on his face. "You'd give it to me?"

"You said we're meant to be together, right?" She arched her back, allowing Ash to slide in even deeper. She hoped it would encourage him to pick up his rhythm again, and when he stayed quiet, she squirmed beneath him. "If we're together, you might as well know my name. It's Calliope. Call me Calliope."

His brilliant sun-colored eyes gleamed. "Calliope," he whispered, drawing back before slamming home again.

Callie grunted, reaching up to stroke the sculpted muscles on his chest. "Oh, yeah. That's so, so good..."

As arrogant as ever, her fae grinned down at her. "I've only just started."

Another squeal as Ash continued to pound her.

Callie hooked her ankles behind his ass, tethering herself to her lover. "Yeah? Bring it on."

She should've known better than to dare him. Because Ash?

He brought it.

AN HOUR LATER, Callie and Ash lay tangled in her sheets, his arm pillowing her, their legs intertwined.

She was finally starting to doze, the endorphins from her last orgasm leaving her comfy, cozy, and satisfied, when Ash cleared his throat. "Callie?"

"Mm..."

"Are you still awake?"

If he stopped talking, she wouldn't be. But since Ash repaid her blowjob by banging her, then going down on her before banging her again, she figured that he had more of a right to pass out from exhaustion. If he was still up, she should be, too.

Her hand slid down his taut stomach, finding the erection that was still hot and heavy against her palm.

Oh, yeah. He was definitely still up.

And she was still humming from his touch.

She scooted closer to him. "Yeah. I'm awake."

"Good. Because I want to give you something."

She nuzzled into his side, lying her head on his

pec, still absently stroking his erection. "You've given me more than enough."

"Let me be the judge of that, Calliope."

She tilted her head back at the sound of her full name. "You remember that, huh?" Their eyes met. In his golden depths, she saw the answer to her question. "Yeah. You remember. What's the matter? It's about time you knew what my real name is."

"It's not so simple as that. Names have power."

"I know."

He arched his eyebrow. "You know?"

"I did a lot of reading after we met. Every book of folktales and fairy lore I could find in the library. If there's one thing they all agree on, it's that names have power. If you give one of the fae your true name, they own you."

"But you gave me yours," Ash pointed out.

"You already own every part of me. My body. My heart. My soul." A tiny grin tugged on her lips. "Might as well have my name, too."

He picked up her hand, lacing her fingers with his. He brushed his mouth against her knuckles, a soft and sweet kiss that was so different than the possessive male that had just boned her nearly senseless.

Different, but still exactly the same where it counted.

"I'll accept your gift, Calliope Brooks. But I've warned you from the beginning, my *ffrindau*. You have the attention of a Blessed One, and I'm not like one of your human males. I accept your gift so long as you accept mine."

There was that word again. He'd used it before and she always assumed it meant friend, but unless he had a habit of sleeping with all of his buddies—and, whoa, was that a thought she didn't want to dwell on for more than a second—then it had to be something else.

Before she could ask him what it meant, though, she realized what he was getting at. And it wasn't the whole "I scratch your back, you scratch mine" thing he had going on. *I accept your gift so long as you accept mine*... it was a fae thing. Never offend one of the faerie races, never offer them thanks, never enter into a bargain with one if you valued your soul, and never expect to have one of the fae in your debt if they could help it.

She gave him her true name. To Ash's way of thinking, the one way to keep the scales balanced would be if he shared his with her.

Callie traced a lazy circle around his dark nipple. "You don't have to do that. It was a gift freely given. I didn't expect anything in return."

"You're mine, Calliope. As your male, it's my responsibility to see that you're never left wanting."

She thought of the orgasms he gave her and barely bit back her throaty chuckle. "You definitely accomplished that."

Ash shifted, using those long, slender, *clever* hands of his to reach down and tweak her clit, sending another jolt of pleasure rushing through her sated body. She would've thought that she was oversensitized by his constant stimulation by now, only this was Ash. His touch did something to her that no one else's ever had—or possibly could.

Callie was as sleepy as she was suddenly turned on. With the sun still streaming in through the slats in her bedroom window blinds, she could tell that it was only mid-afternoon. A short nap to recharge before starting round two seemed like a great idea to her—

—and then Ash slipped two fingers inside of her, testing her readiness, and she figured there would be plenty of time to sleep later on.

Callie let out a soft moan as her fae lover slowly pumped his fingers in and out, in and out. He was teasing her, working her body like this was their hundredth time together and not their first. She had thought that initial orgasm couldn't compare to her addiction of his hands on her skin, and then he blew her mind with the second.

Now, working toward her third, Callie buried her head in the mattress as she lifted up her hips, giving Ash complete access to her body.

He called her his? At that moment, he got no arguments out of her.

She moved with him, meeting his fingers every

time they returned to enter her. He was keeping her loose, keeping her ready, while also teasing her so mercilessly that she would have agreed to anything just to have him trade his slender fingers for the girth of his cock.

He knew it, too. With a smirk that made him seem as dangerous as he was that first night in her kitchen, Ash slowly withdrew his fingers before climbing on top of her.

But, once again, he paused.

She almost screamed in frustration. "Ash!"

"No," he told her, a hint of a tease in his lilting accent. "For you, it's Aislinn. Guard my name. Keep it safe. But know that, whenever you need me, you only have to use it and I'll always come running."

Was it the head of his cock nudging at her entrance that had Callie on the edge of coming? The weight of his fae name settling over her as he easily picked her up by the waist, guiding her to straddle him as he reversed their positions? Or the promise that he was giving her a way to call him since there was no such things as phones in Faerie?

Any of them, she decided, almost deliriously. All of them.

It was all of them.

Callie pushed Ash so that he was lying flat on his back, lowering herself until she was fully seated on his erect cock.

And then, with a smile, she did exactly what he had done when she gifted him with her full name.

She whispered, "My Aislinn," before squeezing his length and starting to ride him.

"It's getting late," his Calliope murmured. "I think the sun's starting to go down."

Ash wasn't so sure he cared. In his more than three centuries, he'd never enjoyed sex as much as he had during the last few hours he spent with Callie. With all of the courtesans who pleasured him, the nixes and the huldra and the banshees he took over his existence, he thought he'd experienced everything his body had to offer. Even the few human females he played with seemed tiresome after a while. When a touch of their hand offered as much of a rush as dipping his cock inside of one, he didn't waste the time getting them undressed.

And then he met his mate.

Callie Brooks.

Calliope.

He let the syllables of her true name echo around his brain.

He thought that the gift of her body would be one he could never match, and while her name hadn't—not quite—it was still pretty close.

But sleeping with Callie? No wonder sex seemed to be so much of a chore after his first century. It was only a warm-up, practice for when he finally found his fated mate, the other half of his soul.

So what if she was human? It might have been a shock to discover the truth behind his attraction to her at first, but Ash was nothing if not sure of himself. This woman—human or not—belonged to him. Of course he took her.

And took her.

And took her one last time for good measure before she finally shoved him away, sleepily telling him she needed a nap.

To his surprise, he fell asleep alongside her. A soldier first, Ash had never slept with another being before; he always slipped out of a lover's bed, careful to watch his back while never letting a conquest think they could take more out of the arrangement than he already offered.

When it came to his mate, though? He would give her everything.

But, in order to do that, he needed his strength. And while he was getting used to spending his days in the Iron, he only retained his power by returning to Faerie before the shadows arrived. He wouldn't die if he lingered, not like how the Dark Fae burned in the sunlight unless they were cloaked in shadows, but he'd be severely weakened.

If Ash was weak, then Callie was unprotected. The bond between them, their fated mate tie was already hard at work. He was a bonded fae male who just claimed his mate. As much as he hated the idea of leaving her bed, putting himself in a position where he could lose her through his own arrogance was even worse.

Swallowing an aggravated sigh, he rolled into Callie, pressing a quick kiss to the top of her pale hair before nuzzling her adorably rounded ear with his nose. "I'd rather stay," he told her.

Even if he couldn't lie, that would still be the truth.

She patted his side. "I know, babe. But don't you have to?"

It all depended on what *have to* meant. To Ash, who would do anything to protect his mate, he decided the answer was: "Yes. But I'll be back as soon as I can."

"Good," Callie told him. Her blue eyes twinkled mischievously. "That'll give me time to miss you."

"You will miss me, Calliope."

"Oh, yeah? Is that a command." She waited a beat. "Aislinn."

He fought the urge to shiver as he heard her use his name. He loved the way it sounded, the way it spilled so easily from her lips, and he wanted to beg her to say it again. It was a brand, a way for her to show her possession of him.

When they first met, he could've used her name to

compel her. But that was before. Now that they were bonded mates, her name was just her name. It was the same way how the Fae Queen couldn't control her subjects by using their true names. He couldn't make his mate do anything she didn't want to, just like how compulsion was just one power that Melisandre couldn't keep after she stole Oberon's throne from him.

There was no time to explain that to her, though. Callie was right. Even if he couldn't see the weak light dribbling through the slats in her blinds as the sun continued to set, Ash's internal clock was telling him to go.

"It's not a command," he said. "I'm just being hopeful that you will."

"Oh." Callie looked surprised. She blinked, then threw him another grin that had his cock stirring. "In that case, I can promise you that I'll miss you as soon as you go."

"I'd stay if it were possible."

"I know, Ash. But, hey. Don't worry about me. Shoot, I might just sleep until I have work on Monday. I'm exhausted."

Ash chuckled as he reluctantly slid out of her bed. "I'll take that as a compliment."

"Do that." From behind him, he heard her voice slur as she swallowed a yawn. "You deserve it."

Bending down, he grabbed his trousers before glancing back at Callie. When he noticed the way his mate watched his naked body move as he started to redress, Ash couldn't help but preen a little. That was one good thing about Callie's sight. When glamour couldn't work on her, her attraction to him held a little more weight. She actually *saw* Ash—and from the scent of her arousal perfuming the air again, he could tell that she really, really liked what she saw.

Damn the shadows. If it wasn't for the dawning night, he'd hop right back into her bed—

No. *No.* He'd return to her as soon as he possibly could. It wouldn't be long, either. Now that she was his mate, his instincts wouldn't *let* him stay away from her.

With one last kiss and another promise to return to her, he used the side of his hand to create four slashes of faerie fire. As soon as the portal appeared, he stepped through it, going from Callie's bedroom to the edge of the veil in one step.

The second his boot fell, he sensed the space in front of him shifting. In an instant, he regretted not taking the portal straight from the Iron to the barracks, but he'd been so careful to always come and go through his post so that the Fae Queen never realized that he was neglecting it while he was with his Callie.

As the Light Fae in the elaborate uniform stepped in front of him, he knew that time—so fluid, so untamable, so unpredictable—had finally run out.

She knew. Melisandre knew.

And she couldn't be happy with him.

Biting back his curse, he bowed his head as he greeted the higher ranking member of the queen's guard.

"Captain Helix."

"Ash." The captain's expression was unreadable as he pulled his diamond-edged sword out from its leather sheath. "Come with me, soldier."

11

Nibbling on her thumbnail, Callie sat on the bench just outside of Buster's. Her sandwich was nestled in her lap, still wrapped up. She had no appetite for the ham and cheese on rye, instead anxiously biting her nail as she tried like hell not to think about Ash.

She never thought he'd be the type to hit it and quit it, but that was exactly what happened. Knowing that days could pass in the human world while it was only a few minutes in Faerie, Callie didn't start to think that something was wrong until two weeks had gone by. The longest stretch of time between Ash's visits had only been about a week and a half, so two weeks wasn't so bad—except she couldn't shake the sensation that maybe he wasn't coming back.

This wouldn't be the first time that a guy stopped paying her any attention after sex. Her high school boyfriend Austin had turned out to be that much of a prick. They dated all throughout freshman and sophomore year, and as soon as Callie let him take her virginity, he dumped her barely a month later. He was already moving onto his next conquest, and Callie learned how to guard her reputation around her judgmental peers.

Since then, she'd been more careful with who she invited into her bed. Ash had three things working against him: he was from Faerie, he was an arrogant bastard, and she knew better than to get involved with a male who had centuries of lovers under his belt. She didn't want to be another notch in his bedpost, and while he told her that he wanted her, that she was meant to be his, it took her much longer to admit that she felt the same.

Whether she should or not was a totally different discussion. The fact of that matter was that she *did* and she wanted so desperately to believe that he was telling her the truth. Sure, he confessed to her that his type of faerie couldn't lie, but a lifetime of dealing with the faerie folk had taught Callie to be cautious. Telling her he couldn't lie... if he could, then that was exactly what he *would* say, huh?

Callie sighed, dropping her hand against her thigh.

She glanced at her untouched sandwich and realized that she had no stomach for it. Wrapping it up, she stowed it in her purse for later, then stood. She wiped her forehead. It was the dog days of summer, early August, and too hot for her to stay outside much longer.

Pity she didn't want to return to her apartment, either. At first, it was because she missed Mitch. Now? She sensed Ash in every corner of the place, remembering the last afternoon they spent together before he, like Mitch, seemed to up and disappear.

But Mitch had at least left her a note. An explanation.

Ash?

He was just *gone*.

Not for the first time, Callie thought about taking a vacation out of the city. If Ash did return to the Iron, his strange ability to find her wherever she was would lead him to the suburbs where her parents and her sisters and their families lived. And if she didn't? She might be able to shake off some of her loneliness while distracting her from his continued absence.

Buster told her she was owed some vacation time. So long as she gave him a couple days' notice, her boss wouldn't mind if she took off a week or so. This time of year business was slow, but it would pick up again come September when there was a rush of clients looking to get all of their summer vacation photographs processed and printed.

She was really thinking that she might. For now, though, she gave up on sweating outside, reluctantly heading back to her empty apartment. Considering her latest ice cream binge, she still had a couple of pints she could tuck into. Might as well grab a container, grab a spoon, and watch a mindless rental video.

Come to thin of it, she never had gotten the chance to watch *Bring It On*.

Just her luck, Blockbuster was out of the cheer-leader flick when she stopped on her way home. She didn't have the heart to grab anything too heavy on the romance, and it wasn't worth picking out a scary movie since that would only remind her of Mitch and Ash. Settling on renting *10 Things I Hate About You*, she thanked the clerk and started the rest of the walk back to her apartment.

By the time she made it home, she was sticky with sweat and feeling a little drained. Tossing her purse and the Blockbuster bag on the back of the couch, she kicked off her sneakers and padded toward her bedroom.

Callie grabbed a change of clothes, then took a quick shower. She brushed her freshly washed hair after she'd scrubbed up, leaving it to air dry instead of bothering with her blow dryer. After shrugging on the fresh tank, panties, and shorts, she went back to the bedroom in search of her slippers.

Surprisingly, the heat was the first thing she noticed. Probably because it was so scorching, it spilled out of her bedroom and into her hall. Her heart kicked up a notch in excitement, hoping that the heat meant what she thought it did and not that her AC had blown another fuse—*again.*

Callie burst into the room, unable to contain her smiling when she saw the fiery Light Fae portal hovering a few feet away from her bed. And next to the portal, there was—

She stopped short, her heart racing even faster as her stomach sank all the way down to her bare feet.

Because the Light Fae male standing, legs braced, hands folded primly behind his back, an unimpressed expression on his blandly handsome face was definitely *not* Ash.

There was something off about him, too. His dark golden eyes seemed spaced a little too much apart, his face pinched, his arms longer than they should be. Callie couldn't see his fingers, but she bet they would be unnaturally long and slender, too.

He was wearing the same uniform as Ash, only his was kind of different. More elaborate, maybe? It had golden thread and an extra row of buttons, she noticed. Did that make him more important?

He was definitely more of a threat.

"Who are you?"

"You may call me Captain Helix," he said, his voice so cold that it was a sharp contrast to the heat causing Callie's damp hair to sizzle. The way he said that made it seem like he was giving her a grand honor to even address him at all.

She didn't know him, but she didn't like him.

"Okay. What the hell are you doing here?" She didn't ask him how he got in—because, duh, portal— but there was no reason he should be in her *bedroom*. Unless— "Where's Ash?"

"That's precisely why I am here. I'm to take you to see Aislinn."

He had his name. This Light Fae who looked so much like her Ash knew his true name.

Did that mean she could trust him? Callie wasn't sure.

"Is something wrong with him? Is he hurt?"

"You'll see when we get to where we're going."

"Yeah? And where is that?"

"My apologies, human," Helix intoned, his cold voice hardening like ice, "if you thought that I would continue to waste my time answering your questions. I've been sent to perform a task. I've been sent by the queen to bring you to Aislinn. You will come with me."

"Oh, yeah. I—"

He drew his sword.

Callie stopped breathing. Just *stopped*. It only lasted

a few seconds before she started to feel a touch light-headed, but even as she stared in ill-disguised terror at the diamond edge of Helix's long sword, any hope that this was a good fae like her Ash flew out the damn window.

Swallowing roughly, she nodded. "Got it. No more questions."

"That's right." He used the point of his sword to gesture to the portal. "Now go before I have cause to push you through myself."

Some part of her had guessed that the portal was meant for her. Up until the moment he waved at it with his sword, she'd hoped that she'd avoid having to take it, that Ash was lost in the human world somewhere and that was why this Helix was there.

Of course not. He never would've stayed in her world without telling her which meant that he was in Faerie—which was exactly where the Light Fae portal would bring her.

During their talks, Ash might not have pushed her to join him in Faerie after her initial refusals, but he made it sound as enticing as he could. She knew that she would be able to enter his fantastical world and, wearing his touch on her skin, be safe from most of its predators. So long as she didn't eat faerie food, she'd also be free to return to her world again, and the worst thing that could happen would be she lost some time.

It could be seconds. Could be minutes. Days. Probably not that much longer unless she spent countless sunrises in Faerie, and even then there was no way to know if she'd lose a year or cross over directly after she would've left.

Trading her focus from the point of his sword to the wall of flames, Callie realized that she would cross over even without the captain's added pressure. Because it had been two weeks of her time since she saw Ash last, and if this fae male was bringing her to him, then he must be in trouble.

Especially since she hadn't missed the subtle way Helix had mentioned the Fae Queen like that.

It's safe, she told herself. Ash promised that he'd seen plenty of humans take a fae portal and they were no worse for the wear. Sure, it was intimidating, but the level of heat she was feeling now was as bad as it got. She wouldn't burn.

Still, as Callie trudged forward, only pausing to slip her bare feet into her ballet slipper-style shoes, she found it difficult to keep her eyes open as she knowingly walked into the wall of flame. She closed them, and swallowed her scream when the sensation was like warm water—similar to her shower—spilling over her, just leaving her dry instead of getting her wet.

It was the promise of seeing Ash on the other side of the fire that kept her walking forward; that, and the memory of the pointed sword that must be at her back.

Only when she felt something solid beneath her feet, the heat blown away by a cool breeze, did she open her eyes again.

Callie jumped. Luckily, Helix and his sword appeared through the portal a few steps behind her so she didn't land on its point—though it was pretty close.

There was another fae male.

For the first time that she could remember, Callie was face to face with one of the Unseelie. It was easy to tell since this male was the exact opposite in appearance to both Ash and Helix. His skin was so pale that it seemed to glow, and he had thick, straight hair cut along his jaw that was as black as night. And his eyes... silver where the Light Fae's were gold, the irises were nearly swallowed up by the whites of his eyes, they were so fair.

There was something else, too...

The fae could never be ugly. They were designed too perfectly for that. But her sight never lied, and there was a darkness in this particular guard that managed to make him appear beastly to her.

She edged closer to the captain and his sword. If it was a choice between being impaled or letting the Dark Fae male get near her, she'd take the hole in her back.

Helix sighed. "That's enough, Dusk. Leave the poor creature alone. Melisandre is waiting for us."

Dusk's mirror-like eyes flashed in something that was malicious amusement. "That she is. Come, human. I see you wear the brand of one of the Blessed Ones. Shame that won't save you."

What?

Helix commanded the Dark Fae to be quiet again and, after that, they both were. All Callie could hear was the pounding of her pulse in her veins and the slapping of her slippers against the crystal floor. She couldn't shake the feeling that she was a prisoner, especially since she was sandwiched by the two very different fae soldiers, and it took everything she had to keep walking if only because she had to see for herself that Ash was okay.

Something told her that he wasn't, and that scared her even more than the Dark Fae in front of her.

They were inside. Callie didn't know precisely where, but since she was heading toward their queen, it was a safe bet that it was her castle. Ash had told her stories about the magnificent castle with its pristine walls and accessories made of crystal. They marched through corridor after corridor, each one more elaborate than the one they passed, until they reached a pair of glass doors guarded by a pair of fae.

Like Helix and Dusk, there was one of each: one Dark and one Light. They wore the same uniform, too, and had a matching sheath hanging off their narrow hips.

Helix said something in a lyrical-sounding language that was most definitely *not* English. The Light Fae guard nodded. As one, the pair of guards each reached for a crystal knob, pulling the doors open for Callie, Helix, and Dusk.

She hesitated when the doors opened, revealing an open room with blindingly white walls, a massive crystal throne up on a six-inch dais, and a crowd full of both Light and Dark Fae all wearing clothes that belonged at a fairy tale ball.

And there, sitting demurely on the throne, sat a female that stole Callie's breath.

She was cloaked in glamour so rich and thick that, even with her sight, Callie saw dainty blonde curls, pale yellow eyes, and perfect, blemish-less, porcelain skin. But because she could *sense* the glamour as much as she could actually see it, she forced herself to look past it. She figured it had something to do with being in Faerie. The powerful magic was working against her human sight, forcing her to see what the female was projecting.

But Callie had twenty plus years of experience. So, knowing she was going to end up with one hell of a headache later, she screwed up her face and *saw*.

Though the glamour would have you believe she was Seelie, the fae female was anything but. The blonde curls turned to long, raven-colored waves. Yellow eyes became dark gray. And the perfect face shifted and twisted just enough to make her menacing instead of innocent.

Callie gulped as the female waved an unnaturally pale hand in her direction. The ruffles on her simple light pink gown moved with the motion, proving she was graceful if nothing else.

As she moved, a male stepped out from behind the throne. Callie's heart leaped up to her throat as she spied Ash—her Ash—wearing the same uniform as always, looking exactly as he had the last time she saw him.

He was okay. This whole strange excursion into Faerie was worth it, because Ash was okay.

She took a step toward him. A warning flashed across his face, there and gone again, but she knew what she had seen.

Callie froze.

"Oh, Aislinn," the fae female cooed, drawing the attention of every being in the room. "My guest has arrived."

And... look at that. She knew Ash's true name, too, thought Callie. Wasn't that interesting considering he made it seem like giving her his name was some grand, important gesture?

And maybe Callie was being catty, but if this was the Fae Queen—and she was betting it had to do because, well, *throne*—then she was the only other woman that Ash offered his loyalty to.

Callie immediately hated her.

The fae female stayed seated on her crystal throne, fingers perched elegantly on the arms of the chair, gesturing at Callie with the curve of her chin. "Tell me. Is this she? The human you've been playing with?"

Playing with?

"Yes, my queen."

"Ugly, isn't she? Those blue eyes and those round ears? Hideous."

Was it possible to hate her even more? Yes. Yes, it was.

"Mm."

"What was that, Aislinn?"

"I said, yes, my queen."

Callie's head jerked toward Ash. Did he just say—

"Ash?"

The queen sniffed. "Quiet your pet, Aislinn. I don't believe I gave her permission to speak in front of my court."

"Silence, Callie."

It wasn't his command that had her losing the ability to speak. It was the cold way he spoke to her.

Ash?

Melisandre preened. "That's better. Honestly, when I requested that you summon your pet for me to meet, I didn't think she'd actually speak to me. Didn't you teach her proper manners?" With a tinkling laugh that left Callie gritting her teeth, the queen said, "Of course not. I can see that you've touched her. Just another human in your bed, Aislinn. Is that right?"

Ash shrugged. He actually *shrugged*. "Blame my post. I got bored. She was entertaining for a time."

"Ah, that's just like you. Always interested in the chase. But once you get your prize... still, I put you at that post for a reason."

"Yes, my queen."

"I should punish you, but you've been a faithful servant to me these last two centuries, so I'll let it slide. In fact, I've relieved you from your post. You join my personal guard at sunrise."

"As you wish, my queen."

Callie had watched the back-and-forth between Ash and Melisandre with a growing sense of horror.

I got bored...

Interested in the chase...

Your prize...

They were talking about her, weren't they?

"What the—" It just burst out of her. "Ash? What's going on? I thought—"

The queen brushed her dark hair over her shoulder. To those who only saw her glamour, it probably looked like her innocent blonde curls were bouncing in place. To Callie, the actual gesture was far more threatening.

"You thought *what*, pet?"

Pet?

Pet?

"Pet?" She turned toward Ash. "I thought you wanted to be my mate. And you're standing there while she calls me your *'pet'*?"

All around her, she could hear the whispers coming from the others in the room. It started when she spat out the word 'mate' and only continued on from there, but Callie droned them out.

Because when Ash answered? She had to hear what he was going to say, even if it broke her heart—

"What was it you said to me once?" Ice. That was pure ice in his voice. "I could lie to your face and you'd never know? Well, human. Now you do."

—and he did.

She stumbled back on her heels. He hadn't reached out and slapped her, but she recoiled just the same.

"What? You... you told me that the fae can't lie."

Ash sniffed. "No. I told you what you needed to hear."

Melisandre clapped her hands. The cracking noise broke the stare between Ash and Callie, drawing everyone's attention back to the Fae Queen.

She rose from her throne. "Aislinn, as your queen, I won't allow this human to treat you in such a manner. I won't punish you. But perhaps she deserves—"

"No." The murmurs of the crowd rose in pitch. It

didn't seem as it was often that anyone dared to inter-
rupt the queen, but Ash just did. "I don't want to see
her punished. Just send her back to the Iron."

Melisandre's pale eyes glittered wickedly. "Only if
you forsake her. With the whole of the Seelie Court as
witness, forsake the human you chose over your
loyalty to your queen."

Choking on her sudden gasp, Callie turned back
toward Ash.

He wouldn't do that, would he? She didn't want any
kind of punishment, but to have Ash *forsake* her after
everything they shared?

For a brief moment, their eyes met, before the Light
Fae looked away.

"You can't forsake what you've never wanted," Ash
announced.

"So be it." With a wave, the Fae Queen gestured to
Helix and Dusk. "There you have it. This human has
no place in my palace or in Faerie. Aislinn said to
send her to the Iron, so be it. I want her gone."

The captain bowed his head. "Aye, your majesty."
With a flick of his wrist, he lifted his sword higher.
"Come, human."

One last look. She gave Ash one last lost, pleading
look, an opportunity to take back everything he said, to
twist his words and tell every fae in the throne room
that he said what he said but it wasn't what he meant.

Only he didn't. The blazing heat that was often there when they locked eyes was eerily missing.

He was a stranger.

Worse, he was everything that she once feared he was and had convinced herself that he couldn't be.

A *monster*.

12

Melisandre waited until Dusk and Helix had forced Callie from the throne room to dismiss the rest of her guard. Taking their cue, the nobles that came for the show all dispersed just in case the queen decided to turn her cruelty on them next.

Though she hadn't charmed him to be a statue, Ash stood still and unfeeling all the same. Only when the two of them were the last ones remaining did he speak again.

His voice sounded hollow as he muttered, "Are you satisfied, Melisandre? I did what you commanded me to."

"Satisfied? You say that like I had you reject your *ffrindau* for my amusement."

Ash could barely find the strength to care that

Melisandre knew exactly who Callie was to him. For days, she pretended that she was insulted that he was caught deserting his post just to entertain himself with a human. She'd acted as if Callie couldn't be his mate only because a human and a fae? It wasn't supposed to be possible.

It didn't matter, though. Melisandre made him a bargain. If he gave up his human, she'd spare Callie's life. Not that the queen needed any reason to just kill Callie—another one of her amusements—but if she gave her word that no harm would come of his human so long as he did what Melisandre told him to, then at least Callie would be safe.

But for Melisandre to knowingly rip two bonded mates apart? That was even more cruel than the rumors in Faerie had given her credit for.

He stayed quiet because if he spoke up again, he'd only do so to curse her.

It didn't matter. The queen wasn't done talking yet.

"You're not the first of my subjects to find their mate in the Iron," she told him, adding salt the his gaping wound. "I gave them all the same choice that I gave you: sacrifice your mating or sacrifice your mate. I can't allow a halfling to be born if I want to keep my throne. You must understand, Aislinn."

He bit down hard, careful to keep his true emotions from crossing his face. A century's worth of habit, of serving under Melisandre and dealing with her fickle moods and her careless whims, and after only a short while with his Callie, he struggled to control himself as she circled him closely.

She was looking for an excuse. Any excuse. If she could find some way that he weaseled out of his bargain, she'd consider it broken and take her anger out on Callie.

Ash would never let that happen.

He should've been expecting something like this to happen. Despite her best efforts to quell any recent discussion of the ancient Shadow Prophecy, the prophecy was as old as time. Only in the last few decades, when the lesser races started to refer to her rule as the Reign of the Damned, did it become clear that it was referring to Melisandre.

> *...a child with powers*
> *part human, part fae*
> *in the Iron,*
> *she's destined to stay*
> *more than a lover,*
> *a consort, a friend*
> *when Dark mates Shadow*
> *the Reign of the Damned shall end...*

When he saw Callie, he saw his *ffrindau*. Uncharacteristically short-sighted, he never thought of the family they might possibly make one day—but

Melisandre obviously had. Any child that a fae created with a human mate would be a halfling.

And a halfling was fated to end the Fae Queen's reign.

It wasn't personal. Ash understood that. She wasn't ripping Callie away from him because she wanted Ash to pay. Any of her subjects fated to bond with a human would meet the same fate.

But at least he managed to save Callie's life. If it meant he was stuck in Faerie forever, eternally separated from his love, he'd do it in a heartbeat.

In Oberon's name, he already had.

Pity the cunning Fae Queen wanted more proof of that.

"Just in case," purred Melisandre before she waved her hand, pulling a patch of darkness toward her.

It wasn't as inky black as the portals some of the other Unseelie made, but there was no denying what it was: shadow magic. No wonder Melisandre had sent the other guards away. She didn't have to worry about Ash retaliating so long as she held Callie's life in her hand; he was no threat to her, and the retinue of guards weren't necessary. She also didn't want any witnesses to her using her Dark Fae powers, not while she still wore the glamour of a Blessed One.

Dipping inside the darkness, she pulled out a wooden box. Erasing the patch with a careless wave, she lifted the lid off the box, careful not to touch what was inside.

Ash knew from his decades working as a guard in one of the infamous Faerie prisons that most of those wooden boxes held pairs of iron handcuffs, perfect to weaken faerie prisoners.

The object inside of Melisandre's box was indeed a set of handcuffs, but these weren't iron.

They were crystal.

"Put them on," she ordered. "Put them on or I have your pet dragged back here again. And, this time, I'll freeze her if I must." For just a moment, Melisandre dropped her Seelie glamour, letting a hint of her feral Dark Fae smile peek through. "I can always use another statue for my garden. The ones I have keep smashing into hundreds of pieces for some odd reason."

Some odd reason? More likely a Dark Fae queen in the middle of a rage.

Ash watched the crystal cuffs twinkle in the bright lights of Melisandre's throne room. Iron cuffs weakened his kind, but crystal? It would keep him from crossing over into the human world ever again.

Just like he thought, he'd be trapped in Faerie forever.

For Callie, he'd give up his freedom.

For his *ffrindau*, he'd do anything.

Ash put on the crystal cuffs.

IT SEEMED LIKE A DREAM, but one that Callie couldn't find a way to escape from.

With Ash's rejection both raw and painful, she couldn't do anything as the pair of fae guards marched her out of the immaculate throne room. The whispers tore at her skin, the taunts and the insults that one of her kind was nothing. *Less* than nothing. She was human, and she never should've looked twice at Ash, let alone believe that he might care for her.

It was all a game, she supposed, her mind a fog as she struggled to keep ahead of the guards and their shiny, pointy swords. The fae did so like to play, and he'd made it clear from the beginning: her sight had interested him, her beauty had attracted him, but it was her refusal to get involved with a creature from Faerie that led him to do whatever he had to to earn her touch.

He was after her soul. Stealing a part of her every time she let him touch her, Ash hungered for the power in her mortal soul. She was the idiot who confused his tenacity for affection. She was the one who brought her heart into it.

She'd loved him. And maybe it was too soon. Maybe she'd let him compel her after all, using his glamour to turn her into his very own plaything. His... *pet*. Ash had vowed that he would never use his magic against her, but if he lied once before, maybe he lied twice. Three times.

Every single time he opened that beautiful mouth of his.

He had sounded so harsh just then. So cold. As he refused her, there was an edge to his musical voice that she'd only heard from him whenever he mentioned Mitch. She had thought he was jealous. Now? Now she knew that, to the Light Fae, her human roommate was just one more obstacle he needed to remove to get at what he wanted.

And he had. She slept with him, letting him touch every last inch of her, and then he was gone.

Time worked differently in Faerie. At least, that's what Ash told her when he explained how days might've passed between his visits when, to the fae, it could've been hours—or it could've been weeks. He promised that he was always working his way back to her, and no matter how long it took, he would return to her side again.

Another promise, she mused as the guards led her down the long stretch of halls in the Fae Queen's castle. Everything was twinkling, nothing clear. She thought it was because the decor was made of crystal, the walls so blindingly white, but as Callie blinked to focus her sight, she realized that she was having a hard time seeing through her unshed tears.

Neither of the guards had spoken to her earlier

except to tell her that she was being brought to Ash. After the queen threw her out of the throne room, the guards stayed quiet so long as she drifted forward with them. She'd take the silence over the arrogant and frosty threats anytime.

She didn't know where they were taking her now, and she thought there should be some relief when the golden guard directed her to another one of the Light Fae portals. She'd never taken one before, and if it wasn't for being told that Ash needed her, Callie wouldn't have ever walked through the one in her bedroom—was it only about an hour ago?

As she stumbled back into her apartment after seemed to sleepwalk back through this second portal, it seemed like it was a whole other lifetime.

She turned on her heel just as the portal winked out of sight, closing off the veil between Faerie and her world—between Callie and Ash.

The pain stabbed anew, the ache cutting through the fog as she began to understand that her trip to the magical realm hadn't been a fantasy. It was real.

And she was changed.

Screwing up her eyes, she looked around her room. She might be changed, but nothing about her personal space was any different. It was exactly as it had been when the Light Fae who looked so much like Ash but *wasn't* waltzed into her private space and commanded her to get decent.

Callie gave her head a clearing shake. It didn't help. She still felt the same sleepy, light-headed sensation that followed her through the two worlds. She had vaguely wondered if it was a side effect of going to Faerie as a human, but if anything it was stronger after her return.

It felt like a dream, but it seemed more like a nightmare.

You couldn't honestly believe that a male like me would want a human like you?

His sneer echoed in her ears. Callie's stomach roiled, the urge to bend over and heave almost too much. Even when Ash made his opinions on humans clear, he'd always implied that she was different. That she was special.

She was an idiot.

Her legs buckled. Luckily, she was near enough to her bed that she allowed herself to drop. To just let go. She sank down on the mattress, blinking rapidly as the tears returned.

He rejected her. Refused her. *Lied* to her. And if he thought she was going to just walk away with her tail between her legs after he pursued her so hard, then he had another think coming. She hadn't had the chance to confront him with the Fae Queen and her entire court watching them. In her space, in her world, she had every intention of doing just that.

But first—

"Aislinn."

The syllables came out softly. *Broken*. It was one thing to muster up the strength to confront him, but her heart was breaking just like her voice.

Callie remained the only one in her room.

It didn't work. Of course not.

Clearing her throat, she tried again, just the way he taught her.

"Aislinn, I command you to appear."

The name was important for a first summoning, Ash had explained in the haze of their love-making, but there was more to it than that. Faerie magic was made up of rules and traditions and instructions that made little sense to the very human Callie, but she accepted it because it was Ash who told her—*and he wasn't supposed to be able to lie*.

She swallowed her pain when seconds, then minutes crawled by and she was still alone. Sitting on the edge of her bed, hands folded between her thighs, she waited. He had to create a portal, she told herself. He said it should be instantaneous, but what if he couldn't get away from the queen?

Aislinn was his name. Callie was at least sure of that. She heard Melisandre use it, and he answered to it. It was his name.

But was it his *true* name?

She didn't know. When it came to the Seelie male

she had loved and lost, it seemed as if Callie didn't know anything.

Three hours after she returned to her bedroom, Callie slowly got to her feet. The tears had dried on her cheeks; with the edge of her fist, she roughly swiped at the streaks. Her head was pulsing. The hazy, dozy dreamlike sensation was gone, replaced by a dull thudding that had her gritting her teeth.

Turning around, she looked at her bed. Three days ago, she'd spent hours wrapped up in those sheets, lying side by side with Ash—plus on top of and underneath, even once straddling his face as he fucked her with his tongue—until he had to leave her right before the sun went down. The sheets still smelled like a combination of sex and her fae lover. Since she hadn't known how long before she'd be with him again, she hadn't changed her sheets just yet. In some sappy, silly way, it was almost as if he was spending the night with her even though he was gone.

But that was before he told her that he got what he wanted, and that she was a fool to think she had anything left to offer him.

Her hands were still fisted at her side. Callie flexed her fingers, trying desperately to push the haughty look of disgust that had twisted Ash's unearthly features from out of her head.

And then, with a yank that sent her comforter and a pillow flying, she started to strip her bed.

EPILOGUE

Ash never came back.

Callie didn't know what she expected.

Well, no. That wasn't true. She just wanted to be proven wrong—and she wasn't.

The name hadn't worked. Deep down, she still harbored the hope that he would pop into her living room, shattering a few light bulbs or shorting out her toaster oven in his wake. With an arrogant tilt of his head and his come-hither smile, he would tell her he still wanted her, that nothing was as it seemed.

Callie held onto that hope for two months. And when summer turned to fall and there was still no sign of Ash, she had to admit that it was time to move on.

So she did.

The first old habit to go was her outside visits. Her

daily trips to the park turned to weekly stops before she gave up on heading to that location. Telling herself that she had plenty of pictures of the trees in their fall foliage—her most recent excuse to go to park and hopefully see Ash—she finally focused on turning her film into prints that might possibly sell. She had thousands of photos from her sessions in the park, and if she needed more, there were hundreds of others she could visit.

If she was lucky, they wouldn't have a tear in the veil like the one near her apartment. No goblins. No fairies. No kobolds.

No fae.

Definitely no fae.

Callie had spent the first twenty years of her life fighting against her sight. It had been too easy to rely on it while she was with Ash, but now that he was gone, Callie went back to ignoring anything wearing glamour. It was safer that way, and after a while she decided her summer fling with Ash was just another in a long line of lessons she'd learned the hard way.

Never trust the fae.

But she *could* trust Mitch.

During her trip to Faerie, Callie lost two whole days, proving that Ash was at least being honest when he said that time moves differently in his realm. Buster was pretty annoyed that she missed a shift, but with a promise that it would never happen again, he let her keep her job. Since she was still concerned about paying all of her expenses without a roommate, she needed to work, and Buster's was the foot in the door she needed for her budding photography career.

Three weeks after she returned from Faerie, though, Mitch showed up at the apartment. With a sheepish expression and an explanation that he obviously doubted held any water, he asked if he could move back in. It had been an irrational, impulsive decision to move out over the summer, but now that he was thinking more clearly, he realized that he wanted his old room back.

Callie of course welcomed him with open arms, though her smile couldn't quite hide her sadness. Because the second Mitch said he wanted back in, she knew for sure that all those suspicions she struggled to bury were true. Ash had done something to her roommate—compelled him, glamoured him, tricked him... *something*—to make him leave. Seeing Mitch standing in the hallway, a duffel bag at his feet, his hand nervously scratching the side of his neck, Callie finally had to accept that Ash wasn't coming back.

Because if he was? Mitch wouldn't be.

Her roommate never talked about his urge to leave after he moved back in. Callie was careful not to bring it up. All too easily, everything went back to the way it was before Ash suddenly stalked into her life at the beginning of the summer. And while little things—the sunshine, a golden chain, even a blown fuse—still reminded Callie of Ash, she got over his rejection because, well, it wasn't like she had a choice.

He might be a powerful, nearly immortal being. Callie was human. She only got to live life once, a measly century at most, and she couldn't waste it mooning over the male she hadn't even wanted at first all because he decided he didn't want her, either.

And maybe she would have been able to fully get over Ash in time—if it wasn't for the fact that he left something behind.

At first, Callie blamed the stress of it all. She didn't have any idea what those fiery portals the Light Fae used to travel between the human world and Faerie would do to someone like her, and causing her to be late seemed like a pretty plausible side effect. After all, she had lost a few days of real life time though she probably spent an hour at most on the other side of the veil. It made sense that it could've done something to her cycle, too.

She figured the first month was a fluke. The second? She started to worry. By the time she hit her third month and she still hadn't had her period, Callie realized that hoping and wishing and praying that she was wrong was just as helpful as ignoring Ash had been once he set his sights on her.

Mitch had been watching her curiously lately, too, which put her back up against the wall. Her jeans felt a little bit tighter, and her hormones were out of whack. When her shoe lace ripped in half as she was tying her sneakers one day and she had a crying fit over it that lasted ten minutes, Callie traded her sneakers for a pair of ballet slipper flats, grabbed her purse, and headed toward the nearest pharmacy.

It was her morning off. No surprise: Mitch was at work, putting in as much overtime as possible in a bid to show his gratitude at his office taking him back after he abruptly quit over the summer. And while her roommate was going above and beyond to make up for his strange behavior—and, likewise, Callie did the same for him since she felt super guilty that Ash had to be responsible for screwing up Mitch's life the way he did—she knew that he would have something to say about Callie buying a pregnancy test.

Like, oh, who could the daddy be?

As far as he was aware—as far as anyone Callie knew was aware—she hadn't been in a relationship since high school. Her last one night stand was more than a year ago. And whether she'd been subconsciously protecting herself or not, she'd kept Ash her very own secret since the fateful afternoon she first saw him in the park.

Of course, there was a good chance she was overreacting. She'd come to terms with the fact that the fae thought of humans as barely more than simple pets or playthings; to Ash, she was a lay he had to work hard for, but the way he pursued her made it clear in hindsight that that was what the fae did. They took what they wanted, and convinced their targets to give them whatever they couldn't take.

If he could get her pregnant, wouldn't he have said something? Or would he have thought she'd consider herself fortunate to bring more of Ash into existence?

No. It couldn't be. A fae sullying his line by reproducing with a human? The arrogant bastard that Ash proved to be at heart would *never*.

Callie clung to that final desperate hope as she tore open the box and read the instructions. A few minutes in the bathroom, then a few more waiting as she paced the matchbox-sized space, all the while assuring herself that it would show one line instead of the dreaded two.

She'd left the tester stick on top of the plastic wrapper, both of them resting on the edge of the bathroom sink. Her eyes were glued to the wall clock, counting down the moments until she could prove that she was worrying over nothing.

Her hands were trembling as she reached for the test. A deep breath in, then a shaky shudder out when the two blue lines stared right back at her from the tiny window.

Callie slumped down on the toilet, the stick hanging limply in her hand.

Pregnant.

She was *pregnant.*

And she had no way of letting Ash know that he was going to be a father.

GLAMOUR LIES

Welp, that's it for the first half of the Callie & Ash novella duet! Thank you so much for reading, and I hope you enjoyed seeing how Riley's parents met— and how Callie discovered that she was both fated to be a Light Fae's mate as well as learning that she was pregnant with Riley/Zella.

Of course, their story doesn't end there, obviously since Callie & Ash are featured in *Favor* (**Touched by the Fae** #0.5) as well as *Touch* (**Touched by the Fae** #3) as a happily mated couple who are desperate to do anything to protect their child from Melisandre, the Fae Queen. So, yes, there will be a second story in the **Wanted by the Fae** duet, coming out toward the end of 2021. Keep scrolling/clicking to get a peek at the cover as well as the description :)

He'll give up anything for her—his home, his pride, his power, his life...

Aislinn has spent his entire existence in Faerie working toward one goal: serving the Fae Queen as a member of her elite guard. Melisandre has had his loyalty for close to two centuries, and even if he didn't agree with her cruelty, she would be his queen until Oberon returned to Faerie and reclaimed his throne.

And then he met Callie Brooks and, suddenly, his loyalty shifted.

The human was his *ffrindau*, his fated soulmate, and the sole female meant to be his. So Ash loved her and he seduced her and, when Melisandre found out and threatened her life, he rejected her.

To save Callie, he had to give her up, and he would've left things as they were if it wasn't for the rumor being whispered in the Fae Queen's Court about a Seelie who fell for a human, and a human who was carrying a halfling child.

His child.

Callie's good at hiding.

Hiding her ability to see through Faerie glamour. Check.

Hiding her heartbreak after Ash betrayed her. Check.

Hiding her pregnancy... Oof.

She knows she won't be able to hide her pregnancy much longer, and when her roommate offers to take on the role of daddy when he finds out, Callie is just glad to have someone on her side. Besides, it's not like the real father is around to help. She might as well tell Mitch yes.

Too bad that Ash has something to say about that when he finally tracks her down again.

At first, she thinks it's because he decided that he *does* want her. But then he starts telling her about something called the Shadow Prophecy and she realizes that hiding her new baby wasn't just a choice.

It was a necessity.

**Glamour Lies *is part two of a duet featuring the very human Callie and the Light Fae male who will give up everything to have her...*

Coming November 2, 2021!

Have you read any of my other *By the Fae* books yet? While, chronologically, Callie & Ash's story takes place first, I already have two complete series that are set both in our world and Faerie:

Touched by the Fae (Riley & Nine)

There once was a prophecy about a halfling fated to destroy the Fae Queen's reign...

Too bad the half-fae, half-mortal woman spoken of in it doesn't know a damn thing about the Shadow Prophecy. But the fae? Courtesy of a mysterious mentor tasked with protecting her, Riley Thorne knows all about *them*.

Because the fae are real. She just pretends they're not.

The Shadow Prophecy is the five-book collection that tells the complete story of Riley Thorne, the daughter of Callie Brooks and the Light Fae Aislinn. It contains *Favor, Asylum, Shadow, Touch,* and *Zella*.

Imprisoned by the Fae (Elle & Rys)

There once was a human woman who accidentally walked through a fairy circle and changed her life...

Elle—at least, that's what you can call her—didn't mean to cross over into Faerie. She didn't mean to eat an enchanted apple and basically trap herself on the other side of the veil. She definitely didn't mean to piss off a Seelie noble and find herself in the most infamous prison in the magical world.

And, most of all, she didn't mean to fall in love...

The Shadow Realm is the five-book collection that tells the complete story of Helen Andrews, a human woman who accidentally finds herself trapped in Faerie. It contains *Tricked, Trapped, Escaped, Freed,* and *Gifted.*

STAY IN TOUCH

Interested in updates from me? I'll never spam you, and I'll only send out a newsletter in regards to upcoming releases, subscriber exclusives, promotions, and more:

Sign up for my newsletter here!

For a limited time, anyone who signs up for my newsletter will also receive two free books!

ABOUT THE AUTHOR

Jessica lives in New Jersey with her family, including enough pets to cement her status as the neighborhood's future Cat Lady. She spends her days working in retail, and her nights lost in whatever world the current novel she is working on is set in. After writing for fun for more than a decade, she has finally decided to take some of the stories out of her head and put them out there for others who might also enjoy them! She loves Broadway and the Mets, as well as reading in her free time.

JessicaLynchWrites.com
cursetheflame@gmail.com

ALSO BY JESSICA LYNCH

Welcome to Hamlet

Don't Trust Me

You Were Made For Me*

Ophelia

Let Nothing You Dismay

I'll Never Stop

Wherever You Go

Here Comes the Bride

Gloria

Tesoro

Holly

That Girl Will Never Be Mine

Welcome to Hamlet: I-III**

No Outsiders Allowed: IV-VI**

Mirrorside

Tame the Spark*

Stalk the Moon

Hunt the Stars

The Witch in the Woods

Asylum

Shadow

Touch

Zella

The Shadow Prophecy**

Imprisoned by the Fae

Tricked*

Trapped

Escaped

Freed

Gifted

The Shadow Realm**

Wanted by the Fae

Glamour Eyes

Glamour Lies

Forged in Twilight

House of Cards

Ace of Spades

Royal Flush

* prequel story

** boxed set collection

Printed in Great Britain
by Amazon